The Wish List Addiction

Lindsey Paley

Published by Prism Book Group
ISBN-10: 194009979X
ISBN-13: 978-1-940099-79-8
First Edition, 2014
Published in the United States of America
Contact info: contact@prismbookgroup.com
http://www.prismbookgroup.com

NOTE FROM THE AUTHOR

This story features 'The Little Green Book of Wishes', a book the main character, Rebecca Matthews, stumbles across when her life is at an all-time low and she is grasping the edge of sanity by her fingernails. Her friends challenge her to make some radical changes to her life.

The book was christened 'The Little Green Book of Wishes' to guide the reader to its inspirational contents. The 'Wishes' have been collated into various sections—'Wishes with Children', Wishes with Partners', Wishes with Friends'—not only for ease of reference but for the reason that we are consistently advised that happiness lies not in the amassing of monetary gain but in the connections we make and sustain with others.

The smallest things can deliver pleasure and cost very little. There is no guarantee that the epic adventure of a lifetime to climb Mount Everest will deliver the dream you have lusted after your whole life, just as there is no guarantee that the homemade play dough won't clog up your plumbing, necessitating a call to the emergency plumber!

'The Little Green Book of Wishes' is not a 'Bucket List' generator—it does not advocate that you draw up a finite list of things to do before you reach a certain age or event and then you can die happy in the knowledge that your dreams have been achieved. Far from it—that's too stressful by half! The risk is that in the strenuous pursuit of one goal and the satisfaction of striking it from your list to move headlong on to the next, the 'Wish List Addict' becomes oblivious to the fact that real life rushes by alongside, which is exactly what happened to Rebecca.

No, this little book of wishes is a 'Dip in/Dip out' book of tantalising gems. It does not contain anything too epic! No 'Round the World Before You're Thirty' suggestions. Try one a week! Try one a month! Challenge your friends or your colleagues to select one for you to undertake at random—the only provisos are that you be safe, do your research and have fun!

See those golden coins of happiness roll in!

DEDICATION

To Les and Ben

Rebecca's 'To Do List'

Pick up dry cleaning (*need navy work suit for court*)

Arrange dental appointment (*mention nagging toothache in bottom left tooth?*)

Arrange optician appointment (*or replace lost arm of specs?*)

Buy milk and bread (*beans/sausages/cereal*)

Ring Dad

Get hair cut (West End salon near work? Maggie's? Local college?)

Write 'thank you' letters to Claudia and Paul (*Too late? Christmas 3 months ago?*)

Buy Helen birthday present and card (*Max's home-made?*) and post (*apologise for not attending party -make* good*, check-proof excuse!*)

Ring bank and extend overdraft

Bake cake for nursery's annual 'picnic-in-in-park' (*buy, then do frosting self?*)

Return library books (*check rules on fines*)

Arrange meeting with Max's keyworker to worrying discuss sleeve-sucking habit (*be strong and assertive*)

Visit possible new nurseries.

Search for Max's health care file then make appointment for pre-school immunisations (*look into purchasing new healthcare file? Research private immunisations?*)

Get Max's feet measured and buy new shoes (*Leather? Trainers? Flip-flops?*)

Ask for time off work for holiday (*a week? a day? finish early on a Friday?*)

Iron clothes (*pay Brittany?*)

Get up earlier!

Rebecca's Wish List

Lose 10 lbs

Learn meditation technique and practice (*short quick lessons with immediate results?*)

Book a vacation with Max (*hotel? self-catering? camping?*)

Look for new job (*more money, better hours, nearer home, less stressful?*)

Spend more quality time with Max and Dad

Move back to Northumberland (*home*)

Register for a First Aid class

Treat self to new shoes (*Jimmy Choos? Louboutins? Nike?*)

Make Scrapbook of Mum's photos and memories box (*for Dad and for Max*)

Join swimming club (*teach Max to swim!*)

Get a pet (*small, check with landlord - goldfish? life span of goldfish?*)

Take Max to the library more often - read more books (*not just Thomas The Tank Engine*)

Get a make-over (*hairstyle? makeup? fitness? therapy? counselling?*)

Date? (*when? how? babysitter? who!*)

Volunteer at hospice (*read newspapers, novels? Offer legal advice - free wills?*)

Buy silk pillowcase (*or demand them back from Brad?*)

Treat self to new underwear (*silk? lace? cotton? market stall?*)

Ride the London Eye with Max (*expensive*)

Fly kite and picnic in park (*free*)

Donate blood (*where?*)

Become a vegetarian (*more healthy/less shopping required?*)

Arrange girl's night out with Claudia and pay

Hire red Morris Minor and take Dad to Church where he and Mum were married (*on wedding Anniversary?*)

Take Max to cinema (*new Disney film?*)

Rebecca's Bucket List

Learn how to make fresh pasta in Tuscany

Learn how to ice-skate

Climb the steps to the top of the Eiffel Tower

Fly in a hot air balloon over the Grand Canyon (*safety? without Max*)

Experience and photograph the Northern Lights

Write memoirs (*or diary/journal/word for the day?*)

Learn to play the clarinet (*like Mum*)

Learn Salsa (*or karate?*)

Be an extra in a movie (*TV? Radio play? Amateur production?*)

Swim with the dolphins with Max

Take Max to Walt Disney World and ride Big Thunder Mountain together

See the cherry blossom spring in Japan (*with Dad*)

Travel by Orient Express from London to Venice

Grow an herb garden (*window-sill?*)

Fly first class to NYC and see a Broadway show (*musical*)

Sponsor a child (*Africa? UK? Mentor a law college student?*)

Visit Rome and throw three coins in the Trevi Fountain

Research Family Tree (*for Dad*)

Find a soul mate (*must adore Max*)

Write will

CHAPTER ONE

REBECCA'S BODY TREMBLED as she awaited the Tribunal's verdict. Her nerve endings tingled with anxiety as her heart hammered against her ribcage. Her future career, her ability to support herself and her son, rested on the stony-faced chairman's next few words. She'd never felt more alone in her life.

"The decision of this disciplinary tribunal is that you be struck from the Roll of Solicitors with immediate effect. You are prohibited from practicing as a solicitor and from conducting any legal services without the express permission of this tribunal. It is a criminal offence to fail to disclose the fact you have been struck off to any prospective employer."

Nausea rose from Rebecca's stomach to her throat. The worst outcome had been confirmed and all she wanted to do now was flee from the chamber to wallow in self-pity, but she was forced to endure the judge's continued ruling.

"The legal profession's most valuable asset is its reputation and trustworthiness, which inspires confidence in members of the public. No solicitor can be allowed to bring the profession into disrepute.

"However, Mrs Mathews, I also have before me an application from Lucinda Fleming of Baringer & Co, seeking permission to employ you in the role of paralegal assistant in their Family Litigation department. This I grant, with the condition attached that you are prevented from the handling of client account monies. You will be closely supervised by Ms Fleming and be subject to monthly reviews of your progress and the meeting of the aforementioned condition.

"Do you understand the decision of this Solicitors Disciplinary Tribunal, Mrs Mathews?" asked the chairman, his well-fed stomach straining the buttons of his pin-striped Savile Row jacket as he leaned forward to peer at Rebecca over his half-moon spectacles.

"I do, sir," Rebecca managed to squeak.

"Do you accept the condition attached to the permission we have granted to Baringer &Co?"

"Yes, sir."

The chairman settled his bulk into the scarlet leather chair before continuing his pronouncement, each word lacerating Rebecca's heart. She struggled not to flinch, drawing in a calming breath which served only to make her feel lightheaded.

"The Tribunal accepts there are no aggravating factors in this matter. No direct financial harm was sustained by any individual member of the public and no client of your previous law firm has suffered any loss as a consequence of your actions. You have been open and honest with the Solicitors Regulation Authority and with this tribunal throughout their investigations.

"Further, we have taken into account that from the outset you have admitted your fault and you have, to date, enjoyed an unblemished career in the law, evidenced by the numerous testimonials before us today.

"However, I'm sure you acknowledge your conduct was irresponsible in the extreme. Whilst the Tribunal accepts you have shown no dishonesty in your actions, you displayed a reckless disregard for the financial consequences of the transaction you concluded, despite it being with the best of intentions.

"My colleagues and I"—he gestured to the stern faces of his two judicial associates flanking him—"trust that with dedication and application in your new role, you will rectify your shattered reputation and discharge your indebtedness swiftly.

"You may apply to the SDT to be restored to the Solicitors' Roll when your bankruptcy has been discharged."

"Thank you, sir."

"Our written decision and reasons for it will be sent to you within fourteen days of today's hearing. I will ensure that Ms Fleming and Baringer & Co receive our written confirmation of the permission to employ you in time for the commencement of your employment on Monday, first April."

"Thank you, sir," Rebecca gulped, tears brimming her auburn lashes.

The chairman noticed her distress and his lined face softened. "I see from your written submission you are recently separated and have a young child?"

"Yes, sir. My son, Max, is four years old."

"Then I am satisfied you will show the utmost commitment to your new post and to your new employers, as failure to do so will leave you in a very precarious position, both for your future career and for your and your son's financial security. I have scrutinised your financial statement and noted you receive no monetary support for your son from your estranged husband. I'm sure you do not need me to urge you to press this matter further?"

"No, sir," replied Rebecca. *Does he honestly believe I haven't sought to do everything in my power to avoid the indignity of bankruptcy?*

"I make an order for a contribution to the applicant's costs in the sum of five thousand pounds, such order not to be enforced without leave of the SDT. You are free to leave, Mrs Mathews."

"Thank you, sir."

Rebecca shuffled together the documents spread over the table in front of her and shoved them into her oversized, black leather satchel. Her stomach dipped and her knees buckled as she rose, but she managed to disguise this on the pretext of grabbing her raincoat from the floor where it lay discarded. Some scenes become seared into the mind's eye, like a snapshot, returned to time and time again. As she glanced back at the bench, she realised this was one of them.

Emerging into the weak March daylight, Rebecca gulped the noxious London air into her constricted lungs, steadying an urgent impulse to vomit.

Ten long years of toil and turmoil in the legal profession, slaving at her desk until the early hours, forfeiting witnessing many of Max's achievements, had culminated in the most devastating thirty minutes of her professional career.

But, she acknowledged, it had been her fault. Her inability to accept there could be no 'Happily Ever After' scenarios for herself and Max had led her to the nightmare of today.

She shrugged into her crumpled Burberry, slung her satchel over her shoulder, and slunk to the end of Farringdon Street to commence the predestined quest of failing to locate an available cab.

She should have predicted her unsuccessful attempt, as well as the ensuing rainstorm, as she dragged out a scrunched up umbrella from the dark recesses of her bag, dislodging a boiled sweet as she struggled to open it in the oncoming downpour.

Changing tact, she made for the Underground at Temple, contemplating her bleak future. Her career was wrecked. It would take years to pay back the money she owed. Whilst she would be eternally grateful to Baringer & Co for offering her a position, she was embarrassed and ashamed of her predicament, anxious about the reactions of her prospective colleagues in the litigation team she would be joining.

Despite her qualms, she was determined to slave her guts out to repay Lucinda Fleming for her generosity. However, she was concerned about how she was going to be able to put in the long hours required to achieve this when she had Max to care for. He had to remain her priority. Nothing else mattered but his wellbeing. Every action she had taken, which had led her to this catastrophe, had been with Max and Bradley's happiness in mind. She'd desperately wanted a better life for all of them, for them to spend more quality time together, in a carefree, less-stressed existence.

Now she boasted no partner, no home, and no career. What a complete failure!

As Rebecca stumbled down the last of the stone steps onto the subway's platform, the jarring of her stiletto heels caused her ankle to twist painfully. Her flesh-coloured stockings splattered with dots of mud, tendrils of her damp copper curls plastered to her high cheek bones, all these woes paled into insignificance when she remembered that the next task on her list was to spill the bad news to her elderly father, who had sacrificed so much for her success and happiness.

CHAPTER TWO

AS SHE PERCHED on the broken plastic seat on the freezing platform, rubbing her wrenched ankle, her mobile buzzed in the deep recesses of the pocket of her Burberry trench, pulled tightly around her waist. Squinting at the caller ID, Rebecca fought an internal battle whether she had the stamina to undergo a second intensive interrogation that day.

She'd spent the whole morning enduring the embarrassment and humiliation of being lectured on how her professional life and legal career now lay in tatters, emerging with no doubt she was a complete and utter failure.

Could she tolerate being ridiculed and scorned further—reinforcing how her personal life was a disaster, too—especially by her estranged husband of all people? Well, in for a penny, in for a pound, as her beloved mum had been fond of repeating whenever Rebecca had been stubborn in her refusal to progress with anything too challenging. A clash of intense pain in her abdomen reminded her of the gaping hole the loss of her mother had left in her life, an emotion she had experienced every day of the last five years.

She depressed the call accept button. "Hello, Bradley."

"Rebecca, I wanted to know the outcome of your disciplinary hearing." No niceties, straight to the point.

"As expected. Struck off. The Tribunal had no other options." She paused for his response. Nothing. "Thanks for asking. Yes, I'm devastated. I'm soaked to the skin, I've a sprained my ankle, and I'm freezing my butt off waiting for the tube."

She slouched lower, hugging her satchel closer to her body for its non-existent warmth.

"No sympathy from me, Rebecca. You've only yourself to blame. It was a ludicrous decision to buy a tumbling down old wreck of a cottage in the back of beyond. Who in their right mind would consider relocating from the bright lights of London to the wilderness of Northumberland? I still cannot fathom out what possessed you to do it!"

"We've been through this, Bradley. I am under no illusion whatsoever regarding what you think of my decision-making abilities." She lifted her dark auburn curls from her pale face, running her frozen fingers through to the ends.

"If only you had discussed the matter with me first, Rebecca, you could have avoided this whole fiasco. It was an outrageous presumption on your part. Did you honestly envisage me living amongst the country folk? Tweeds and wellies? You're even more insane than I gave you credit for! That I would trade in my Porsche for a Range Rover and take up grouse shooting? Crazy, delusional woman.

"And the fact you even contemplated I would give up my fantastic career. I am close to making partner at Studley Smith, which will mean mega-bucks, and will get me a new, more spacious apartment, maybe overlooking the Thames this time. I'm thinking minimalist, clean lines, flooded with natural light, no clutter or any of those garish soft furnishings you are so fond of! Onwards and upwards, Rebecca. Work hard, play hardball. Enjoy the success—don't let anyone or anything get in your way, that's the motto I live by. It's worked for me, and I'm just about there.

"But look at you. 'Think of others', 'be caring'—that mentality sucks. It's weakness and look where it's got you. You're a spectacular failure, you know that!"

Rebecca had endured his soliloquies before. She screwed up her eyes and braced herself for his next barbed attack, which always inflicted the most pain.

"If only you hadn't gone behind my back and got pregnant, we could have been living the dream together. Great careers, fantastic opportunities, fancy cars, the X-factor lifestyle, exotic holidays, like Jonathan, and Scott, and their partners. We're all off to Bali in June. But, oh no, Miss 'Happily Ever After' family girl wanted to rush off and build her cosy home. I'll never forgive you, Rebecca. Never. I didn't factor a family into my lifestyle and you knew that.

"Well, you've made your nest, as they say. Now you have to live in it. And if you dare have the audacity to ask for child support again, now that you have purposely sabotaged your career—firstly by having an unwanted child, then by the outrageous stupidity of purchasing a dilapidated cottage thereby causing your own bankruptcy, and secondly getting yourself struck off the solicitors' roll—then you are even more idiotic than I initially thought."

Rebecca tucked a coil of auburn hair behind her ear. She had never been able to fight her corner when facing an onslaught from Bradley, but even peering out of her pit of darkest despair, she could not allow him to get away with that disgusting insult.

"Max is not an unwanted child. He has a mother and a grandfather who love him with all their heart and soul. Not having either of the latter, Bradley Mathews, you are totally unable to appreciate that."

Bradley was more the type to work on his external attributes. Immaculately groomed, clean-shaven, short dark brown hair clipped every Saturday morning, golden tan, professionally applied, well-cut, dark charcoal suit, and the obligatory crisp, white cotton Jermyn Street shirt, double-cuffed to display his huge collection of whimsical cufflinks. Only highly shined, Italian leather shoes were acceptable for his baby-smooth, pedicured feet. He even had a signature scent, Chanel's 'Pour Monsieur,' liberally applied.

"Well, just don't expect me to come to your rescue with any cash. Cheryl and I will be forking out for completely new wardrobes for this trip to Bali. We'll need a couple of treatments as well, so we are buffed and bronzed before we hit the beaches.

"I had no hand in the embarrassing predicament you find yourself in. I am ashamed to admit to my friends and colleagues what has happened. I hope this doesn't filter down the legal grapevine!

"Why don't you sell that God-forsaken place in Northumberland anyway? Soon as you do, you'll be able to reimburse your father and settle the ill-advised loan which caused this nightmare. Your bankruptcy would be discharged and you could then apply to be reinstated on the Roll."

"Rosemary Cottage *is* on the market, and you already know that! It's been on the market for the last seven months. But the roof needs patching up, the gable end caved in during the February snow, and the recession is biting hard in the northeast. If I could sell the place I would!"

Rebecca watched as a tube train slid into the station. Commuters swarmed on, but she let it pass, not wanting to continue the discussion in front of an audience. She swapped hands, plunging her frozen fingers into her pocket.

"Just proves my point, don't you think? Who in their right mind wants to live up North? Do they even have theatres in Northumberland? Art galleries? Celebrity chef restaurants? Designer clothing boutiques? Isn't it all racing whippets and peeing on leeks for the men and the Women's Institute and knitting tea cosies for the women?"

Rebecca had heard all the insults before. Even when they'd been together, before Max had arrived on the scene, as a glittering, high-living young professional couple with the legal world their oyster, Bradley had insisted on deprecating her northern roots. She no longer rose to the bait—if it wasn't for Max, she'd relocate back north in the blink of an eye.

Twirling a thick strand of her now-dry amber hair around her index finger, she doggedly pursued her futile goal. "Will you come and visit Max this weekend? He'd love to spend some time with you."

"Can't. Me and Scott are off to Brighton for a stag weekend. Marti's getting hitched at the end of April, the mug. There're twenty of us dedicated to giving him a riotous send off. Look, Rebecca, I'm going to be busy for the next few weekends. Got an invite to the company's corporate box at Stamford Bridge. Fantastic opportunity to network. Need to bag a couple more high-profile clients. So I won't have much spare time. Anyway, why are you eternally hassling me about this? Am I one of your 'to do' items on that infuriating bucket list of yours? What is it? Persuade Bad Bradley to step up as a father?"

"But you haven't seen him since Christmas. Come with Cheryl, take him to the park for an hour or so. Surely you can manage that? Please, Bradley. He needs to know you're around."

Every conversation they'd conducted, some more cordial than others, over the last two years, had culminated in a plea from Rebecca for Bradley to spend time with his son. Each time Bradley produced an elaborate excuse or a blank, unexplained refusal. He had no interest in anything beyond expanding his materialist empire and experiencing as many exciting moments as he could cram into his luxurious lifestyle. In his view, Max was her son, not his. But, for Max's sake, Rebecca had to keep on trying and it was for this reason she remained in her tiny, dingy flat above a flower shop in Hammersmith.

"Maybe I'll have some time free in May before we fly off to Bali. I'll ask Sonya to check my diary and get back to you—see what I can fit in."

Rebecca's heart ached for Max. She found it increasingly difficult to stomach these familiar arguments with Bradley about maintaining contact with his son. No more arrows remained in her quiver of persuasion. Every ounce of her energy had drizzled away leaving an exhausted, empty shell.

"Bye, Bradley."

Rebecca contemplated the filthy black rail tracks below her, her body trembling from the temperature and the conversation. If it wasn't for Max…

From the moment he had burst into her life, she'd loved him with an intensity she'd never experienced before. Bradley had refused to attend the birth, so her best friend, Claudia, had travelled to London to perform the role of birthing partner, bringing with her a wealth of experience and her wicked sense of humour, having produced three delightful children of her own.

When Max had been handed to her in the operating theatre, his green eyes—precise replicas of her own and his grandmother's—his spiky tufts of hair identical in colour, not ginger but the colour of a fox's coat, she knew she would fight to her last breath to protect him and make him happy.

What a failure she'd been in that department. Since Bradley had abruptly informed her that he could no longer endure the chaos, surrounded by the paraphernalia of an inquisitive toddler, Rebecca had striven to perform the dual role of mother and father whilst holding down a full-time job as a family litigation lawyer at Harvey & Co.

Max attended Tumble Teds nursery, conveniently located in a huge Victorian terrace house at the end of their street, run like clockwork by Barbara Babcock, a matronly woman Rebecca struggled to like.

Max hated it.

It broke her heart every morning when she dropped him off on her way to work, seeing him standing there at the bay window, waving goodbye, his cherubic little face clouded with sadness at seeing his mummy walk away, a weak but brave smile fixed like glue on his pinched lips.

He was always the last child to be collected at the end of the day. Mrs Babcock often scolded Rebecca for arriving beyond their closing time, a privilege for which she received a monthly invoice. Bradley had never once dropped him off nor collected him, even when they had been together.

Rebecca had queried with Max's keyworker—for that was what his allocated nursery nurse was labeled—why his sleeve ends were always soaked when she eventually did collect him. She was informed Max spent the whole day chewing the ends of his sleeves despite being gently persuaded not to do so.

[12]

It tore Rebecca's heart out, but she had no other choice whilst they lived in London, initially because their mortgage had been so huge it required two incomes to service, then later to allow Rebecca to pay the hefty rent on the drab flat in Hammersmith. She spent every weekend making up for Max's week at nursery—swimming together in the local pool, going wild at soft play, attending Sunday school at the local church, and scampering around the local park until Max spotted a dog. Energetic or lethargic, toy-size or extra-large, he was equally terrified of them all.

Rebecca was aware of the solution to a more balanced, carefree life, but things hadn't materialised as she had intended. She'd dreamed every day during her filthy, skin-crawling commute to work of relocating to Northumberland where she'd grown up, running wild in the fresh, clean, crisp air, swinging from trees, paddling in the steams, building dams. But it was this 'pie in the sky' dream which had led to the destruction of life as she knew it.

When Bradley had persuaded her to sell the matrimonial home, having his own clandestine agenda for doing so, Rebecca had made the most outrageously ridiculous decision of her calm and ordered life—to purchase a gorgeous, stone cottage in the pretty village of Matfen in Northumberland.

Rosemary Cottage, complete with ivory roses climbing high around the front porch, was the precise embodiment of her intricately woven childhood fantasy. She'd fallen in love with its symmetrical proportions as soon as she'd laid eyes on the place, taking leave of her senses—again. She'd decided to buy it on the spot, and the complicated scheme she'd dreamt up in order to keep the transaction a secret from Bradley until she could unveil it in all its splendour as the answer to their failing marriage had exploded spectacularly in her face.

CHAPTER THREE

MONDAY, APRIL FIRST. Rebecca's first day at Baringer & Co. She'd taken extra care to tame her fiery curls into an elegant up-twist secured with her favourite tortoiseshell clip. She's chosen to line her striking eyes with a swipe of jade eyeliner, and a slick of pale peach lip gloss completed her beauty routine. She'd mined her closet for her plainest black trouser suit and flat pumps, hoping to be able to blend into the background. A spray of Chanel No 19 behind her lobes gave her neglected self-esteem a nudge.

Predictably, April had opened with one of its renowned showers as Rebecca and Max scuttled down the street huddled together under her flimsy, old orange umbrella.

Max had been more clingy than usual that morning when she'd dropped him at Tumble Teds. The previous evening, as they snuggled together under his Thomas the Tank Engine duvet, his soft, smooth body emitting her favourite aroma of baby shampoo, Max had confessed to her that a boy at nursery, Stanley, was mean to him. He'd followed this night time disclosure up the next morning with a query as to why he still had to go to nursery when Rebecca knew Stanley would be horrid to him that day.

The guilt! The self-awarded badge of 'dreadful mother' worn today next to the shiny new one proclaiming 'new girl' sealed her trepidation for the day ahead. She'd be Rebecca Mathews, nee Phillips, neglectful mother, lowly paralegal at Baringer & Co, as opposed to Ms Mathews, senior litigation solicitor at the prestigious Harvey & Co.

Keep to the newly drafted 'to do list for failed solicitors', Rebecca. Keep your head down, your record impressive and any remaining ambitions out of sight. You need to keep this job, and the alterative would be dire, she told herself. She was determined to repay Lucinda Fleming's generosity with hard work and gratitude, never pushing beyond her perch on the lowest rung of the legal ladder.

All spare time had to be spent in the office, repaying her debt of appreciation, or at home making it up to Max for the enforced nursery attendance. *Focus only on your goal to pay down your huge debt, repay Dad, and the bank and get back on the solicitors' roll.* A Herculean task for someone as prone to failure as she! But she had to achieve this, to provide a future for Max.

There would be no socialising with her colleagues. No dissecting the day, gossiping about difficult and ungrateful clients over a relaxing spritzer in the wine bar after a hard day's slog.

As she approached the impressive offices of Baringer & Co, she reconsidered her internal arguments. Who would want to befriend her anyway? A failed, struck off, disgraced solicitor. Shame spread through her veins, heating her pale skin to the roots of her already escaping curls. For what she had put herself, Max, and her father through, how could she ever atone for their disastrous misplacement of trust?

She rode the elevator to the twelfth floor and gave her name to the glamorous receptionist—Victoria Munro, her name badge announced in the corporate colours of Baringer. Then she plunked down on the black leather sofa and prepared to meet her doom.

CHAPTER FOUR

LUCINDA FLEMING STRODE toward her. Rebecca had met her before as a fellow court advocate, but never on her own territory. She was tall, slender, and exuded elegance. Her perfect, honey-coloured bob swung smooth and glossy, ending at a sharp right angle to her chin. Her long fringe skimmed her precisely defined eyebrows, not a single strand out of place. Involuntarily, Rebecca smoothed her tumbling curls behind her neck and drew herself up a little straighter.

"Rebecca, come this way, please. I'll direct you to where you will be working." No pleasantries offered, no acknowledgement they had previously been acquainted, frequented the same court corridors, and even knew some of the same people. Rebecca's spirits sank further into her sensible ballet flats. Why hadn't she selected her favourite designer nude stilettos? They would have increased her height and confidence.

She trailed in Lucinda's wake down a long glass corridor in the slipstream of her rich exotic perfume. What perfume was it, Rebecca wondered, preferring a lighter fragrance herself, one that incorporated the clean, tangy aroma of citrus and fresh cut grass.

Lucinda's rear view was as sharp and sophisticated as her front. Four-inch, black stilettos. Wow! Were they Jimmy Choos? Shapely stockinged calves, well-toned buttocks clad in a thigh-hugging, black pencil skirt skimming her knee, no shorter. A beautifully cut, matching black jacket nipped in her narrow waist. Her shoulders held erect, head high, oozing confidence and self-knowledge. Whilst Rebecca couldn't hope to compete with Lucinda in the style stakes, she did regret not making more of an effort.

"This will be your work station. We operate a clear desk policy at Baringer & Co. An inspection takes place every evening. Please, do not place items of personal adornment on the desk. You will ensure your computer is switched on by eight forty-five at the latest each morning and that it is not closed down until five thirty p.m. at the earliest. Baringer & Co demands a high level of commitment from all its employees, from the mail girl to Mr John Baringer himself.

"Training sessions take place on Wednesday evenings or Saturday mornings, which you will attend with your team. You will also be expected to represent Baringer & Co at all networking events. The terms and conditions of your employment with us as a paralegal are contained in this arch lever file. Study it. If you have any questions relating to the contents, e-mail me. Please, sign and date the acceptance document at the front and return it to me by Friday.

"Now, here's your headset. Deborah Bell"—she gestured to a harassed-looking young woman in the next booth without meeting her eye—"will assist in getting you up and running on the computer. Your performance will be reviewed on a monthly basis, in addition to your adherence to the conditions laid down by the SDT." Her tongue sharpened around the diatribe of the issued instructions.

Leaving Rebecca cringing at the public announcement of her disciplinary shame, Lucinda strode away, her impeccably chic figure disappearing into her prestigious corner office, no backward glance, not even a departing smile to crack her severe expression.

Rebecca watched as Deborah too scrutinised Lucinda's retreating rear, as though marveling how she made walking in four-inch heels look so graceful and refined, before skidding across to Rebecca on her desk chair's wheels, her long, pale blonde waves swishing across her pretty face.

"Hi. Ignore her. We all do, don't we, Nathan?" she called over to a skinny, hunched, twenty-something man, who raised his head to Deborah, pointing emphatically to his headset, whilst manically flicking his pen between the fingers of his left hand.

"Call me Deb. Ms Ice Maiden didn't introduce you."

"Rebecca Mathews," said Rebecca and she stuck out her hand.

Deb considered Rebecca's proffered hand, her pale sapphire eyes taking in her tight, nervous face. "Well, let's get you set up. Nathan'll bring us coffees when he's done with his client." Deb lifted her ample bottom from the scarlet desk chair and bustled like a mother hen around Rebecca's desk.

She must be five years younger than me, thought Rebecca. Feelings of inadequacy coiled around her abdomen as Deb set up her computer and showed her the various programs they used, chatting and smiling all the time. *How does she get to be so cheerful?*

"I'd like to report that her bark is worse than her bite, but unfortunately it's not true. I'll warn you now, Becky, she's a top-notch ego-breaker, just ask Nathan." Deb chuckled. "Cruella de Vil

[19]

eat your heart out, Lucinda Fleming's after your reputation! Just be on your guard, that's all I'm saying, especially if you are the chosen target practice for the week. Her arrows are sharp and travel straight to the heart."

Deb zoomed her outstretched index finger into her ample breast spilling from a low cut, deep magenta, shift dress stretched to its limit, her laughter lighting up her pretty round face sprinkled liberally with freckles, her mischievous, clear blue eyes crinkling in the corners.

"Married to the company, she is. She's in the office before any of us drag our weary bones in here, polished to perfection. Have you seen her manicure? What I'd give! She's always the last to leave, unless she's off to a conference or a lecture. Take her threat of the clear-desk policy seriously, too." She glanced at her own cluttered desk. "Been reprimanded lots of time myself. Tidiness is not one of my fabulous attributes.

"She's an impressive advocate, though. Butters up her opponents and then, zap, goes in with the carving knife when their back is turned. Her success rate is second to none. Even John Baringer is in awe of her. She earns oodles of money for the firm, so she gets away with her lack of personnel skills with us minions. I'd hate to be up against her in court, not that I ever get to go to court—too lowly, even to carry her briefs!" Deb giggled again as she placed a yellow legal pad and a set of Baringer & Co pens in front of Rebecca.

Nathan finished his call and slung the headset down on his desk, leaning back in his chair almost horizontal, running his surprisingly large hands through his spiky dark hair. Only ten o'clock and his red corporate tie hung loose around his scrawny neck.

Deb made the universally recognised sign for coffee and he trotted off like an obedient child.

"Just beware, Ms Fleming can be vicious. Oh, I don't mean in any physical way—that's not her bag. She takes profound pleasure in emotional and psychological abuse—a well-timed derogatory remark to keep you on your toes. She knows everything that goes on here, and possesses an elephantine memory which stores up misdemeanours to be recalled whenever we need to be reminded of our lowly credentials."

She counted on her fingers. "Don't be late, ever. Don't leave before five thirty unless you are attending a networking event, and then don't leave until at least nine p.m. Don't ring in sick, ever. And worse of all, if you've got kids, don't be off if they are sick. No family-friendly, work-life balance policy here at Baringer & Co. Ms F doesn't have a family. She was grown in a lab. Nor any friends either as far as we can tell—not even a boyfriend!" Deb's eyes widened with horror. "So she sure isn't going to make any allowances for a sick child.

"'Baringer & Co must be your priority, Miss Bell.'" She performed a perfect imitation of Lucinda's stern, haughty voice. "If you want to progress at Baringer you must be dedicated and focused on one goal only—its success!"

Deb plonked her voluptuous bottom back onto her swivel chair and shuffled back to her desk, replacing her headset. "Good morning, Baringer & Co. How may I help you?" Red Baringer pen poised, she scooped her tumbling hair away from her smiling face and behind her surprisingly petite ears.

Rebecca experienced a stab of panic in the pit of her empty, rumbling stomach as she sipped the welcome cappuccino delivered by Nathan. Max wasn't a sickly child by any means, but nursery was a breeding ground for industrial strength viruses. What if he

[21]

became ill? She had no back up available. Bradley wouldn't help. He was made from the same mould as Lucinda—strapped to the treadmill of corporate advancement to the exclusion of all else, snotty, germ-ridden little boys in particular.

Well, stick with the 'new career' to-do list, she told herself. Head down, work hard, ask no questions, and follow the rules. She glanced at the bulging red arch lever file left by Lucinda on her desk. Finally, pray to the God of single, working mothers everywhere—that Max steered clear of the rampant nursery bugs. Could she send him to Tumble Teds in plastic medical gloves?

More worrying though was the demand she be involved in regular networking after work. Nursery ended at six thirty prompt and she had no regular babysitter to call upon. Her neighbour, Brian, a single father himself, had occasionally taken Max and his daughter, Erin, to the cinema and she'd minded Erin, a cute five year old with a mild Barbie addiction, in return.

And training sessions scheduled on Saturday mornings? She and Max had an unbreakable pact to spend Saturday doing fun stuff. She was grateful for the job, to be able to provide for herself and Max, and needed to keep it desperately, but it was going to mean huge sacrifice on both their parts, and the impact would fall most heavily on Max. There'd be no Sport's Day attendance this year, or end-of-year presentation, his last at nursery before starting school in September. But if she didn't go, he'd have no one to watch as he performed his role in the presentation.

They were no different from many families struggling to balance their commitments. Family and friendly were two words totally absent from many legal firms' vocabulary and rarely present when tied together. Baringer & Co was not unusual or any more miserly than others. Wealth and ambition were the only two words worth pursuing to achieve career success in the legal profession.

That's why I'm such a failure, Rebecca mused. She needed to change her vocabulary.

CHAPTER FIVE

LUNCHTIME AT LAST. Rebecca darted to the ladies' room. She hadn't had a chance to read the rule book on toilet breaks so had endured a screaming bladder until lunch.

Returning to her work station to collect her trench coat, rain was still lashing down the windows. Deb was waiting for her, her own trench—a lime green and pink blossoms affair—pulled tightly around her waist, clutching a sunshine-yellow umbrella.

"Me and Nathan usually grab a sandwich at our desks, but in your honour, we'll show you one of our favourite lunchtime haunts. Got your brolly? It's still bucketing down."

Deb led her and Nathan to the local café where they settled on tall leather bar stools facing the steamed up windows streaming with rain, hugging their coffee mugs with both hands. Glancing at the expanse of thigh revealed by Deb's crossed shapely legs, Rebecca was at last grateful for her conservative choice of a plain, black trouser suit.

The café was populated by other escapees from the daily grind, their damp, grey faces testament to the necessity to abandon the desk chairs for a resusitory mug of decent coffee before the challenge of making it through to five o'clock.

"How was your weekend, Nath?"

"Rotten, as usual. I'm considering giving up the fight, Deb. If it wasn't for me mam, I'd slink off into the clouded black horizon. Emma's dating a new guy, so it's back to square one."

Nathan hunched his thin, bony shoulders as he sipped his scalding black coffee. From this angle, Rebecca noticed his protruding ears made his drooping face more hangdog. She smiled at a fellow, well-used doormat.

"Nathan's got a little girl, Millie. She's three and so cute you could just eat her up," Deb explained. "But Emma, that's Millie's mum, is a tyrant of the highest degree. You know she is, Nathan! She refuses Nathan contact with Millie, usually when she has a boyfriend in tow. When did you last see Millie, Nath?"

"Christmas, but that was just so she could collect her presents."

"Nathan's tried everything. He pays child support every single month, never misses. He texts every Friday without fail to find out if Emma will agree to a visit. He sends cards, letters, and pictures. But Emma only agrees to let Nathan see Millie when she's not got a man in her life or when she needs some extra cash. Millie loves seeing Nathan, but it's been three months since the last time and he's terrified she'll forget who he is."

Deb placed a gentle hand on Nathan's skinny knee. "Maybe now's the time to take off your kid gloves, Nathan, and get a solicitor involved? Eh? Lucinda'd whip her into shape—I'd fold at just one glance. Don't be such a defeatist, stand up for your rights. And Millie's rights, too!"

"Won't work, Deb. And this new guy is scary. She met him at the gym. Rugby player, six foot four, and works out every day, she informs me." Nathan visibly cringed.

"Like I said, I'd abandon all hope, but mam isn't responding to the treatment, maybe only has six months at the most and she's desperate to see Millie before, well, before…" He cleared his throat. "Well, she can't travel, not from Edinburgh anyway. I asked Emma if she'd agree to let me take Millie up at Easter, but she flatly refused. Spending time with Rugger Boy."

Rebecca smiled at Nathan's downcast eyes. "I know how you feel."

Nathan raised his head, a skeptical look in his dark eyes. No you don't, it said.

"My situation is different, of course. The complete opposite, really. I've got a little boy. He's four. His dad refuses to see him. I've tried everything, but Max doesn't fit into his high-flying, luxurious corporate lifestyle. Max wouldn't reflect well on his fastidiously groomed, playboy image." Rebecca knew she sounded bitter, but she didn't intend to.

"Well, if you ask my opinion, and I know you didn't—who would? But I'd give up. I've been trying to persuade Emma to agree to regular contact for the last two years since we split and it hurts like crazy. I'd have called it a day ages ago for my own sanity if it wasn't for me mam. But she won't be around forever, so I'm carrying on 'til…well 'til the end. But *you* can just forget it. Don't inflict the pain on yourself or Max." His black eyes sparkled and Deb deftly changed the subject.

"Anyway, guess what? I'm getting married. In October. Look!" She flashed her emerald and diamond engagement ring shaped like a daisy, wiggling her finger under Rebecca's nose. Rebecca noticed Deb surreptitiously cast a glance at Nathan.

[26]

"Oh, it's gorgeous! Emeralds are my favourite, too." It proved to be the right thing to say, allowing Deb to launch into a new topic of conversation.

Flicking her damp blonde hair behind each ear, she fixed her willing audience with her azure stare, her face alight with excitement. Nathan rolled his eyes at Rebecca, but shrugged his shoulders and leaned forward.

"We've—that's Fergus and me—we've been saving hard for four years now. We're having the biggest and best wedding ever. We're being married by Reverend Briggs at our local church, St Mary's. He's even allowing us to recite our own poems to each other! Then, it's off to Radley Hall for the reception. I adore Radley Hall. Me and Alison, my sister, enjoyed a spa day there at Christmas and it's so awesome. It's a dream come true to hold our reception there—that's why it's taken so long to save for our wedding. But it'll be worth it.

"I've chosen my dress, it's adorable. I'll show you the design when we get back to the office. Its ivory taffeta skirt is overlaid with tulle, which is scattered with satin petals around the hem, the bodice embroidered with tiny sea pearls.

"Ooooh, and the flowers. We're sorting them out next weekend. I'm thinking deep purple Calla Lilies. Calla means beautiful in Greek, did you know, mixed with velvety mulberry and cream roses.

"Mum and Gran are baking the wedding cake themselves, but I'm taking evening classes in sugar craft so I can ice it and design the decorations myself.

"I still need to find shoes, though. Can't wait to go shopping for them. Did you know Jimmy Choo has a bridal range? They are to *die* for. Will you come with me, Becky, one lunchtime? Try some on? The boutique's just along Sloane Street.

[27]

"I need another visit to Harrods, too. Oh, no, I'm not buying anything there, far too expensive, but it's the most fab place for ideas for this season. Fergus says you only get married once, so make it as spectacular as your wildest dreams. You'll love Fergus. He's my George Clooney. Fergus Andrew Horne.

"I'm having four bridesmaids and two matrons of honour. I've chosen this stunning royal purple taffeta for their dresses, think deep rich merlot wine, and that'll be our colour theme. I'm dieting hard, need to lose a few pounds, but Fergus loves me how I am—curvy." She ran her hands down her ample body, stretching the hem of her shift dress down toward her knees only for it to ride straight back up her thigh.

"Honeymoon will be a surprise though. Fergus and his dad are sorting that out. Somewhere romantic but hot—it'll be October!

"We've got a deposit saved for a house in the same street as my mum and dad. Nothing on the market yet, but old Mrs Granville'll probably need to go into a care home soon, so we'll wait and see." She chuckled as she drew in another breath. She was so upbeat Rebecca could almost hear the drum.

"Anyway"—Deb blew out her cheeks in an effort to calm her excitement—"I hope you settle in at Baringer & Co. Me and Nathan'll watch out for you. What've you got planned for the weekend? Fancy a trip to Harvey Nicks? I want to test out their bridal makeup, get my eyebrows done, and maybe get a manicure. My older sister, Alison, is coming, too. Go on, a girly shopping trip will do you good!"

With a final sip of the bitter dregs in their coffee mugs, they jumped down from their stools, anxious to get back to their desks before the two o'clock deadline.

"I'd love to, Deb, but I can't. Sorry. Max has a birthday party for one of the kids at the nursery he attends." Rebecca grimaced.

"Pirate theme. Costume obligatory. Max is really excited, but I overheard the boy's mother worrying about whether the party bags were adequate as they only contained a video game and a Harrods teddy bear as she couldn't afford Steiff! For twelve four year olds! Max would be happy with a packet of sweets and a slice of birthday cake. I can't even afford the birthday gift for little Ptolemy, so Max shouldn't even be going. But he pleaded to go as he and Ptolemy share an intense love affair with Thomas the Tank Engine and his friends. Bradley doesn't pay child support," she added by way of explanation of her impecuniary to her new confidantes.

"That's completely abhorrent. You should consult a solicitor, too!" said Deb, chuckling at the irony. "Hey, actually I can help you there. Alison gave me a book token for my birthday last month. Thinks I'm ancient at twenty eight. Crazy girl! She knows I don't read anything except glossy bridal mags and I've got all of them. It's been languishing in my desk drawer ever since. Why don't you take that and get Ptolemy a book? Kids love books. Anyway, who in their right mind calls their child Ptolemy?"

"Oh, that's really kind, Deb, but—"

"No. It'll fester in the wasteland of my bottom desk drawer if you don't. Please, take it! Why not buy yourself a book, too, a good romance, cheer yourself up?"

They shuffled into the glass elevator, umbrellas dripping into puddles on the pale marble floor. Deb jabbed button number twelve.

"Well, I *have* spotted this fab book—last week when Max and I were browsing and coffeeing in the local independent book store, Charlie's. Its title is *The Little Green Book of Wishes*. Max adores books, especially Thomas and his Friends. We could both happily relocate our sparse possessions and take up residence in that bibliographic maze of paradise.

[29]

"I have to confess a middling to severe addiction to drafting 'to do' lists. Got a list for everything and every occasion, you name it, stoically slogging my way through never, ever reaching the end. Sometimes, I don't even remember why the item is on the list at all! I have daily 'to do' lists, well-researched 'wish lists', and also a master 'to do' list—the infamous 'bucket list'. My list addiction was the source of many a jibe from Bradley when we were married. He even cited it in the divorce papers as one of the grounds of my unreasonable behaviour!

"Conversely, this little gem of a book challenges the reader to discard those mocking lists that are never completed and to use its suggestions or guidance *ad hoc*. A sort of lucky bag of wishes you can just 'dip in, dip out' of over weeks and months with none of the stress of fretting about when the next task on the bucket list will be achieved, so you can tick the box and hurtle onto the next. In fact, it positively encourages you to expel the lists from your life in favour of the more random approach.

"Going cold turkey and ditching my innumerable lists, including my painstakingly researched bucket list of fabulous but unattainable dreams, which I have to add, I've only just stuck my toe into, is the stuff of nightmares. My lists are my life's structure— their removal will bring my carefully crafted walls tumbling down around me.

"But then, despite all the meticulous mapping, there are so many areas of my life I've botched up. Career—fail. Money—fail. Property—fail. Relationships—fail, Sports—fail, Hobbies—well I don't have any so you could count that as a fail. The list of a total loser!

"For a failure like me whose recent self-centred mantra seems to be 'I wish...' well, *The Little Green Book of Wishes* is the perfect bedtime read!"

They settled into their respective cubby holes, swiftly typing in their passwords to restart their time recording clocks—every single minute had to be accounted for at Baringer & Co. Deb bent over to rifle through her cluttered bottom drawer, favouring Rebecca with a full display of her impressive cleavage.

"Right, here's the token. Fifty pounds? Will that be enough? Buy the 'Wishes' book and bring it in next Monday. The only condition attached to my generous gift to you is that you agree to me and Nath dipping into its confetti of wishes and not to duck out when we throw them in your direction!

"List making is banned," Deb went on. "It'll be just a random selection from each section! There will be no ultimate goal, only to have fun. Each challenge will be marked out of ten. We'll transform you from a fragile failure to a sparkling success." Deborah grinned with a wicked glint in her eye.

Ah! What had she done?

CHAPTER SIX

"COME HERE, MAX. What about this set of Horrid Henry books for Ptolemy?" Rebecca suggested as she and Max browsed the brightly coloured, crammed shelves in the local bookshop. "Is Horrid Henry cool? Look, *Horrid Henry Meets the Queen, Horrid Henry's Birthday Party, Horrid Henry Tricks the Tooth Fairy.*"

"No, Mum. Ptolemy only wants *Thomas the Tank Engine* books," Max said, dragging Rebecca by the hand to where his trained eye had located the books of his idol. "These are the best books ever! Can I have one, too?"

Rebecca crouched down to Max's eye level and flicked through the book he had selected, watching his cute, eager expression as he agitated at her side.

"Please, Mum, please? Percy's my absolute favourite. But Henry and Gordon are Ptolemy's favourite."

She checked the price on the back of the chosen, must-have book—two pounds ninety nine.

"Yes, love, you can have this one. What about a box set of ten different engine stories for Ptolemy?" Would that be adequate compensation, she wondered, for the party bag containing a coveted video game and a Harrods teddy bear? Twenty five pounds? Should she select some sweets, too? Or was sugar a banned substance?

She popped the set of books under her arm and grabbed Max's hand. "Can we just have a look at the books for Mummy, please? I've seen a special little green book. Can you help me find it with your sharp eyes?"

"Wow, like a treasure hunt, you mean?"

"Yes, come on."

They weaved their way up and down the bibliographic labyrinths in their quest for the hidden treasure. At last, Rebecca spotted its bright emerald spine. Only one left on the shelf. She experienced an inexplicable stab of relief and then joy.

"*The Little Green Book of Wishes*. Over here, Max!"

"I'll help you pull it out, Mum. Oh, there's no pictures inside. Are you sure this is the right one?" Max crinkled his nose in puzzlement.

"Well, that doesn't matter, sweetheart. I love it! Look." She flipped through a few pages for Max. "It's got lots of suggestions for wishes we can try out together. There's even a special section called 'Wishes with Children.' How about we create our own gooey, coloured play dough and design a model for Granddad's mantelpiece? Want to have a go at that?"

"Yes, yes, yes."

"And what about we have a go at producing these fabulous musical maracas, or this cardboard kaleidoscope and daub them with bright paints?"

"Yes, yes, yes."

"It's a deal. Come on then, let's pay the lady."

She produced the book token and handed it to the bored, unresponsive teenager behind the cash desk at Charlie's, silently launching a prayer of thanks in Deb's direction for her act of generosity which had produced so much excitement for Max and herself, even to the extent of allowing Max to attend Ptolemy's much-anticipated pirate party.

"When can we go to the party, Mum? Is it nearly time?"

"Not yet, sweetie. Let's go grab some orange juice and a cookie. I'll wrap the Thomas and his Friends books and you can write the birthday card for Ptolemy. We'll transform you into a pirate in the restroom before we go. Then off we sail to the pirate bash."

"Yes, yes, yes."

Oh, for the boundless energy of a four year old! But Max's enthusiasm rubbed off on Rebecca as they plopped down into a huge, overstuffed leather sofa at the coffee shop next to the bookshop. Dividing an orange juice and a packet of shortbread between them, they poured over the trials and tribulations of Thomas and his right-hand engine, Percy, while Max snuggled into the crock of her arm.

"Don't forget we're travelling up to visit Granddad straight after the party, Max. Do you promise to be a good boy in the car? I know it's a long way, love, but Auntie Claudia'll be waiting for us when we arrive and you'll be sharing a room with Harry on the Thomas blow-up bed! He'll be fast asleep when we arrive, but you can play with him in the morning when you both wake up."

"Yes, yes, yes."

Bless him. I love him so much, thought Rebecca, as she slowly turned the colourful pages, her heart swelling at his simple joy as each new picture of Thomas, Percy, Gordon, or Henry was revealed, the anticipation of his friend's pirate party lighting up his face.

[34]

Children never saw beyond the immediate. If it was her, she'd be complaining like mad about being strapped in the car for a three-hundred-mile journey that could take six or seven hours depending on such unpredictables as the weather and the traffic.

I desperately want a better life for him, she reproached herself. *He needs to spend more quality time with his only parent.* Rebecca had noticed he hadn't once chewed at his sleeve that morning, barely able to contain his happiness and excitement, full of bounce. She hoped his arch-enemy, Stanley, wasn't going to be at the party to spoil his glow.

I need to get out more too. Deb's right. Move on with my life, meet new people, if not for my own sake then for Max's. I'd be happy never to date again, but I realise I have to escape the rut I've carved for my non-existent love life. It was so much easier not to bother. But how was she going to meet anyone? When did she have the time to meet anyone? Where would she go to meet someone?

Leaving Max to peruse his book, she located her own choice from the toast-coloured hessian bag. She stroked its cover. Emerald green *was* her favourite colour—was that a positive sign? Just the title promised so much. It could have been written especially for her, a confirmed wish-list addict. Would its message of 'ditch the list' deliver the catalyst for more focus in her life where the obsessive list making had failed? How could the performance of random acts, undertaken purely for themselves, win over a life plan of structure and a clear focus on the achievement of goals? Reluctantly however, she had to admit that her obsession with lists had delivered her nothing but abject failure when she undertook an honest dissection of every area of her current life.

She parted the tightly packed pages at random, the sharp crack of the spine and the fresh new book aroma she loved permeating

[35]

her nose. It wouldn't just be a lucky dip barrel for herself, but one Max could be part of, too.

The book was divided into five main sections. In addition to the 'Wishes with Children' she'd seen earlier, her eyes were drawn to the section entitled 'Wishes With Your Partner'. The bold heading was followed by five sub-sections, the first of which caught her scouring eye—'Meeting'. Perfect choice for every single mother's lucky dip wish! The narrative included a star rating system to warn of the ease or difficulty in achieving each wish. Three stars! Well, the author had not promised or guaranteed any of the inclusions would be a doddle to fulfill.

She skimmed the page of advice. *There is no way I can do any of that. Mmm? No, I'm not confident. No, I never initiate a conversation, especially with strangers, and no way is my body language interesting and receptive. My use of eye contact is usually minimal and I have no attractive qualities or self-esteem to display to a possible subject. Wow, and this is only three stars out of a possible five! It should be five!*

But there was one thing in the advice section she could do, rarely undertaken these days though. 'Light up your face with a smile!' *Right, this book cost me—sorry, Deb—ten pounds and I owe it to her to give it a go.*

"Come on, Max, sweetheart. Let's get you ready for the party."

"Yeh!"

Max's short legs, now encased in the obligatory red and white stripped uniform of any self-respecting, fashion-conscious pirate, took a flying leap from the deep recesses of the leather sofa as Rebecca finished shoving his clothes into her trusty black satchel. She gathered their bags, plastered a smile onto her pale apricot lips, and swerved it towards an unsuspecting bearded guy reading *The Daily Telegraph* by the exit.

He stared at her for a frozen moment, a fleeting flash of fear darting through his hazel eyes, and then he buried his head back into the quivering travel section.

Well, that didn't go too well—but early days. Would she have more success with what Deb and Nathan selected for her on Monday?

CHAPTER SEVEN

STUFFED FULL OF birthday cake and e-numbers, Max bounded out of the Viceroy's suite of the Grosvenor Hotel having proclaimed to have had 'the best day of his whole life.' He clutched his pirate booty party bag, the size and weight of a small briefcase, to his chest with his plump little hands, excitement and exhaustion battling for victory.

"Can I open it now, Mum?" asked Max, trying to peer inside the sealed bag.

"Just wait 'til we get you to the car, eh? Then you can empty it out and not lose anything or get it wet." She and Max sprinted into the ceaseless drizzle to where she had abandoned the car to a parking meter at enormous cost.

Securing her dripping russet locks behind her ears, she bundled him into the booster seat in the back of her ancient silver Mégane, taking extra care to ensure he was securely fastened in for the long, tortuous drive to Northumberland. She prayed he wouldn't throw up after all that party food he'd devoured and the violent shaking when he'd followed the snaking conga around the hotel's corridors. The thought of the sweet aroma of vomit wafting in the car for the next seven hours didn't bear thinking about.

She'd trekked to the North East so many times in the last six months that she was acquainted with every bathroom stop between London and Newcastle intimately. She planned to break the journey at Donington Park Services to change Max into his pjs and hoped he'd sleep the rest of the way.

"Are you excited about seeing Auntie Claudia and Uncle Paul? Rowan, Harry, and Daisy will be fast asleep by the time we arrive, but you'll see them at breakfast."

"Okay, Mum. I love Harry, he's so cool!"

Harry was Claudia's middle child and only son. Now five, he attended the local primary school which Max thought was awesome. Rebecca could already see that he would grow into a very handsome young man, reflecting his father's Italian heritage—tall, olive-skinned, mischievous dark eyes.

All three of Claudia and Paul's children were delightful, well-mannered, well-brought up. No angst in their family, just plenty of mutual love and affection, time for fun and games, but with an expectation of respect for each other and the world.

Rebecca loved the time she spent with her oldest friend. She and Max were always made to feel part of their extended family whenever they visited—much more frequently at the moment since her father had had his stroke.

The clouds spilled their contents, inundating the motorways with treacherous driving conditions and slowing their progress on the long journey, causing them to arrive even later than expected. When they did pull up at the cheery crimson door of the huge Victorian stone semi, Claudia was waiting anxiously at the bay window. She rushed out to help with their bags and to carry a snoozing Max upstairs, depositing him on the blow-up sleeping bag on Harry's action-figure-inspired bedroom floor.

Despite the late hour, Claudia looked fabulous. Regardless of the fact she had three young, lively children and a husband with a stressful career, her long mahogany hair hung sleek and glossy like wet tar, her straight-as-a-die long fringe skimming her kind, chocolate-brown eyes. Even at eleven o'clock at night, her full lips wore a bright scarlet cupid's bow, a stark contrast to her porcelain skin. She hugged Rebecca warmly, emitting the faint cotton-wool smell of baby talc.

The pair had been best friends since middle school, maintaining their affection even after Rebecca had disappeared to chase the bright lights and toxic fumes of London. Rebecca knew who had made the better choice.

"Leave the bags and come sit in the kitchen. The aga is still warm."

The fragrant aroma of garlic wafted through the cluttered farmhouse-style kitchen. No sleek, minimalistic lines here. Rebecca's stomach growled loudly as she perched at the scrubbed pine table, covered in the remaining debris of the family's supper, and she realised she'd eaten nothing since the corner of chocolate birthday cake she'd shared with Max at the motorway service station.

"I'll just pop up to the bathroom. I feel so grimy." She checked on Max, blissfully asleep in his blow-up bed, performing a stranglehold on his beige, curly-furred teddy bear, Ptolemy's party-bag gift.

Rebecca returned to the kitchen, slumping down at the scrubbed table, as Paul produced a goldfish bowl sized glass of rich red Merlot—her favourite.

"Mmm, I needed that." She smacked her lips, savouring its velvety smoothness as the nectar slid down her throat, spreading its rejuvenating warmth around her jangling veins. "Thanks for doing this, Claudia, I really appreciate it."

Claudia dished up a large helping of homemade lasagne, pushing a pink-spotted cream bowl filled with watercress salad toward her.

Claudia's kitchen was cosy, no other word for it. The room embraced her, cocooned her from all outside anxieties. When the kids were around, it was the hub of the home, the engine house, noisy, chaotic, but still exuded warmth and security. It was Rebecca's favourite place in the world at that moment in her life and she truly hoped she would be able to recreate this ambience in her own kitchen one day, maybe at Rosemary Cottage.

No, that wasn't a dream she could allow herself to place on 'Rebecca's wish list'.

"Don't keep thanking us, Becky. You and Max will always be welcome here. That's what friends are for." She plonked into the wooden chair opposite Rebecca, sipping her own, smaller glass of Merlot.

"You look exhausted. Eat up and then get some rest. I've made up the sofa in the lounge for you. Beware though, Rowan, Harry, and Daisy know you're coming, so be prepared to be bounced awake!"

Rebecca savoured every mouthful of the delicious pasta—there was never homemade cuisine in the Mathews' household—and drained the last drop of wine from her vase-like glass. Like Max, she was asleep before her head hit the pillow.

"AUNTIE BECKY, AUNTIE Becky. Wake up, wake up. We've got a pet rabbit. Come and see him!"

Yanking her fluffy white robe across her body, she was dragged outside to meet Mopsy, the black-and-white dwarf rabbit. Max, still in his pjs, hung back slightly, clinging to Rebecca's sleeve, his fear of all creatures great and small postponing his introduction to 'Magpie Mopsy', as Paul had christened her, in deference to his favourite football team.

Harry, his dark, spiky hair in tufts, having met no comb since his pillow, liberated the squirming rabbit from her hutch, offering her for Max to stroke.

"She won't bite you," Rowan reassured a wide-eyed, hesitant Max. At eight, she was a miniature version of Claudia—delicate features, huge chocolate-brown eyes, poker-straight, chestnut hair, a little shorter than Claudia's mane but with the same full fringe skimming her long eyelashes. Like her mother, she was blessed with a sweet-tempered nature and the uncanny ability to accommodate a nervous disposition, soothe frayed nerves, and encourage confidence.

Rowan calmly stroked Mopsy's silky fur, smiling encouragingly at Max. Glancing up nervously at Rebecca, Max reached out the full length of his arm and ran the tip of his index finger down Mopsy's quivering spine.

"She's so smooth and soft," whispered Max, his eyes wide.

Claudia wandered out with two mugs of steaming brew into the toy-strewn, child-friendly garden, complete with cornflower blue and clotted cream wooden playhouse-cum-storage shed, adorned with daisy-sprigged, pastel bunting, flapping in the gentle April breeze. Thank goodness, the rain had taken a day off.

"You get off to visit George, Becky. Paul and I'll take the kids swimming. Harry can do a whole length in the big pool now, can't you, pet?" She gently patted down his messy tufts as Max moved to a full hand stroke of Mopsy's velvety coat. "He wants to show off to Max."

"Thanks, Claudia. How is Dad?"

"I called in on Friday with Daisy after *Mister Jingle Jangle*. George loves Daisy. Well, they all do at St Oswald's Lodge. He's frail, but his mind's bright as a button. Try not to worry, Becky, you're doing all you can. It's hard being so far away."

"I should be here for him, Claudia. Should visit every day. After Mum died I only managed once a month, if that—Bradley hated the journey—until he had his stroke before Christmas. With everything that's happened, I feel so responsible."

"I know you do." She laid her arm across Rebecca's thin shoulders. "But you must stop punishing yourself about the money. It doesn't help anyone."

"But it's my fault he's in St Oswald's Lodge. He should be with us, or in the lap of luxury at Morningside Towers, living out his twilight years with an onsite cinema, a swimming pool, and a spa, for goodness sake! Even a chiropodist and a hairdresser visit weekly. I wanted that for him, Claudie. He's worked hard all his life and he deserves it."

Rebecca swallowed a rising sob—mustn't cry in front of the children who were now running and screaming around the garden. Pulling herself taller, she took a disguising gulp of her cappuccino.

"There's nothing wrong with St Oswald's Lodge, Becky. Your dad's happy there, they treat him well, and you know that. Anyway…" She grinned, returning to the chaotic kitchen to prepare bacon sandwiches for everyone. "What would your dad have done with a swimming pool and spa? He's not up to diving in the deep end. And a hairdresser? Well, with the greatest of respect to George—not a regularly required service for him, is it?"

[43]

Rebecca returned the smile of her dearest friend, surveying Max and the Scott children from the kitchen window as they chased the hopping rabbit around the neatly trimmed lawn, and sighed.

"I know, I know. But as soon as Rosemary Cottage is sold, the first thing I'm going to do is pay off the outstanding fees at St Oswald's Lodge and move him to Morningside Towers."

Claudia removed her well-used, orange cast iron frying pan from the cupboard and busied herself with browning the bacon for sandwiches.

"What's happening with the cottage, Becky?" Paul probed, appearing at the door fresh from the shower, the spitting double of his five-year-old son—same dark, handsomely etched features, same untamed espresso hair, his slender body encased in fitted black jeans and navy hoodie.

"Absolutely nothing. No viewings since February when the roof tiles on the gable end collapsed into the back bedroom under the weight of all the snow. The garden's a tangle of wild flowers and overgrown herbs. Who's going to take that on, even though it *is* right next to Hadrian's Wall? Even an avid historian would draw the line at a horticulturist's worst nightmare! I don't have the finances to repair the roof nor the time to spend clearing the garden. But until the work is done, the property is not going to attract any serious buyers, I'm afraid.

"I'm desperate to get it sold though, Paul. Jeremy Goldacre, the estate agent who's handling the sale, advised me to reduce the price again. But I've already reduced it by thirty thousand pounds, and if I reduce it any further there won't be enough to repay Dad what I owe him and the bank loan I took out to discharge his outstanding care home fees at the Lodge. And they're *still* in arrears."

Rebecca twiddled her empty coffee mug, staring at the remaining dregs, as Paul slid next to her at the huge pine table. "I

[44]

should loathe that cottage. Its purchase caused this miserable nightmare. But every time I visit, even with the questionable charm of its crumbling roof, I fall in love with it again. It's exactly the home I dreamed of when I was a girl. No Barbies and dressing up in pink netting tutus for me. Climbing and swinging from trees, constructing pebble dams, exploring the fields with the boys, building dens out of knotty branches and hay were my chosen leisure pursuits!

"I dreamt of the exact replica of that sturdy stone cottage, pale ivory roses arching over the front door which had to be dead centre, windows divided into four panes either side and upstairs in perfect symmetry, nets wafting in the breeze, white picket fence, gate slightly ajar. The garden filled with cute pink fuchsias—still my favourite—wild swaying grasses and sweet-smelling herbs emitting their fragrance as you brush past them along the cracked front path, and heavily laden fruit trees in an orchard at the back. Listen to me, I've missed my vocation, should have been an estate agent. I'd make a better stab at the job than Hurray Jeremy!

"But it's not just the property, Claudia." She paused to accept the deliciously fragrant bacon sandwich and douse it in HP sauce. "It's what it promised—a better quality of life for Max, with Dad, you, and Paul on the doorstep. Max attending the local village school and inviting his friends 'round to play. With the countryside offering an extension of the garden, the opportunity for Max to run wild and free in the fields of the farm next door, just like I did, would be so good for his wellbeing. Enjoying the cows and sheep, not terrified of all animals, no matter how small and placid, not cooped up in a tiny, grotty, overheated flat above a flower shop, hating the horrendous hours he's forced to spend at nursery. You know, he's the last child to be collected on an evening? How can I do that to him? He doesn't deserve it. I'm a rubbish mother."

[45]

This time she couldn't prevent the lone tear trickling down her cheek, watching it splash onto the worn, bleached table. She brushed others away crossly.

"I should never have bought it, I know. I got carried away, surfing a wave of nostalgia. I should have consulted Brad first. But I so wanted it to be a surprise for him—a packaged solution to our problems. Dad was all for it, bless him. He's always wanted us back here, couldn't fathom the lure of London. I get that now.

"He was an angel, lending me the money. But I should never have accepted it—it was everything he had, Claudie, every penny from when he sold the barn after Mum died.

"But the biggest mistake was putting his name on the deeds, just to keep the purchase a secret from Brad until I could reveal the cottage in all its glory. I'd have wrapped it in a red ribbon if I could! Then, after the unveiling ceremony, me and Brad could have raised the mortgage and paid Dad back with any interest he'd lost. No harm done. I didn't for one minute pause to consider the consequences, nor did I have any inkling Brad would drop the bombshell of his affair and walk out on us.

"Then Dad had his stroke and couldn't stay in his supported flat, even with the daily carers coming in. And to cap it all, he has to pay full fees there because he owns a property and assets worth more than twenty-three thousand pounds!

"I'm a useless daughter for not forward planning for my own dad's future. I have even less of an excuse with my renowned addiction to list making. Oh, don't get me wrong, I did have a very comprehensive list, but, obviously, it omitted to include the scenario of my husband dumping me in the mire!

"Oh, yes, and add to that lengthening list a rubbish friend, too, who dumps all her woes onto her undeserving friends. I'm so grateful to you and Paul for accommodating me and Max, and for visiting Dad at the Lodge with Daisy. He loves your visits, you know."

Claudia stroked Rebecca's pale, limp hand, as Paul tended the second frying pan of sizzling bacon for the kids' breakfast, its pungent, mouth-watering smell drawing the children in from the garden.

"George does worry about you, Becky. He needs to be reassured you are happy and settled before he goes. He knows you're not and it upsets him. Have you told him you've been struck off because of the bankruptcy? That you lost your job at Harvey & Co?"

"Goodness, no! It'd kill him. He and Mum made huge sacrifices to send me to uni. I miss Mum so much, Claudie—every day. I wish she was here, just to give me a hug." She couldn't prevent the hot tears any longer.

Paul refilled the kettle and set it to boil, bustling off to round up the children and start the delicate negotiations of persuading Daisy to get dressed in something other than her favourite candy-pink tutu and princess tiara for their trip to the pool.

"Come on, have a hug from me." Claudia, familiar with mopping up tears on a daily basis, reached across the table to wrap her arms around Rebecca's slumped shoulders. "You know, this addiction to list making has to stop, Becky. Don't take this the wrong way, but could your blinkered focus on achieving a directory of desires have made you forget to simply live and enjoy life, or to deal with whatever life throws in your path when fate chooses to fling it your way?"

"Claudie, as usual you are spot on. I am obsessed with the hope that, with the structure of a written list, my life won't go off piste. But it's taken some very hard lessons for me to realise no matter how many lists I make, no matter how successful I am at achieving the tasks, life is uncontrollable—well, mine is! But I'm terrified to ditch my lists, Claudie. They are the lifebelt I cling to in the raging storm which is my life right now."

"You've certainly had your share of trauma, Becky. Anyone who's endured the turmoil you have would experience the same crisis of confidence. But, you know, avid concentration on an unachievable bucket list risks neglecting the challenges of the present, those little things that bring us tiny nuggets of happiness, regular doses of which provide contentment and the strength to press ahead. You do realise that a bucket list is a roll-call of experiences to do *before you die*! Not in the next six months! You've got all the time in the world to climb Kilimanjaro, or whichever mountain you've got on that infuriating list."

"It's Mount McKinley." Rebecca giggled, for the first time hearing the stupidity of her obsession when all around her, life as she knew it, was crumbling. "Well, you will be relieved to be informed that I intend to do just that. Ditch the list!"

"Deb and Nathan, the colleagues at work I told you about, have also confronted me with my obsession, which culminated in me indulging in the purchase of a book entitled *The Little Green Book of Wishes*. I must confess, I did initially intend to use it to draft more lists—but only of the wishes variety, not the bucket variety," she hastily added, glancing at Claudia's scowl. "But the note at the front from the author clearly directs the reader to use the book as a 'lucky bag of wishes', to dip in, dip out of its gems of advice, and discard the stress-inducing, must-achieve bucket list. What better self-help tome is there for a girl like me? I'm Rebecca Mathews, nee Phillips, and I'm a listoholic!"

Claudia smiled at her best friend. "Why don't you grab the bathroom and take a leisurely shower, use the expensive stuff Paul bought me for Christmas, on the glass shelf above the bath. Don't

[48]

understand why I guard those shiny bottles so slavishly, except they do look too pretty to use. Go on, we'll sort Max out with his breakfast and swimming gear. You get off to visit George. Send our love and warn him I'll be down with Daisy on Friday. And don't fret, Becky. He's happy there!"

CHAPTER EIGHT

REBECCA POINTED HER old silver car into the terracotta-coloured gravel parking bay, crunching to an abrupt halt. She was anxious to spend as much time with her father as she could on this visit. She knew he missed seeing her and Max immensely, but not as much as he missed the company of his beloved Marianne.

Since his stroke at Christmas, he had steadily become more frail. Although he still clung to all his faculties, his memory was fixed on the past, not the present. When she visited, they spent their time together reminiscing about her happy childhood, laughing at the antics she had performed, her rejection of all things girly for the freedom and adventure of running wild in the meadows surrounding their converted barn, her Titian hair flying in tangled ringlets behind her.

They always chatted about her mum, sometimes as though she was in the next room, recalling the forty-five years of happily married life George and she had enjoyed, an accolade Rebecca would never match.

"Hi, Dad." She found him sitting in his wheelchair on the patio in a sheltered spot, wrapped in an emerald and black tartan blanket, his unlit pipe clamped between his teeth, the smell of dried tobacco sending ripples of childhood nostalgia through Rebecca.

"Becky!" Raising his frail hand in greeting, George removed his pipe and placed it carefully on his blanket-wrapped knees. His bright blue eyes sparkled at her arrival. She bent to kiss his papery cheek, tucking the blanket more securely around his immobile legs. "No Max?"

"He's gone off swimming with Claudia, Paul, and the kids. I'll bring him in after lunch."

"Lovely, pet. Shall we decamp into the lounge? It's getting a bit draughty out here now and there's tea and homemade cherry scones on the go. You're too thin. Do you eat?" He repeated the same admonishment every time she visited him.

They settled into the peaceful, chintzy residents' lounge, the April sun's weak rays catching dancing dust particles. The aroma of home-baking permeating the room, as a huge green teapot and a stacked plate of well-risen cherry scones were deposited on the smoky glass coffee table by a chirpy young Polish girl.

"Just a cup of tea for me, pet. You be Mum!"

Rebecca only just managed to grip onto her wrecked emotions, as her weary mind leapt to the gaping hole the departure her beloved mum had left, her pain still raw as she sat pouring tea for her dad as her mother had so loved to do.

"How's that job of yours? You work too hard for that company, you know. I hope they appreciate you."

"I know, Dad."

"Well, you need to start thinking of that young lad of yours, before he starts reception class in September. You don't want to be sending him to an inner city school in London. When are you moving back up here? Living in that cottage you bought? The local village school only has sixty kids, you know. He'll love it. He'll get all the care and personal attention young children need there, a more rounded education than just cleverness from studying books.

"I want to see you settled and happy, Becky love. I know you and Bradley weren't able to mend your differences and I'm sorry about that, but you and Max have to come first now, not Bradley. That's why you're sticking things out down in London, isn't it? So he can be near his dad? But what about all the other positive reasons for moving back up here? Remember your list addiction, Becky? Pros and cons? You need some joy in your life. I see none in your face."

He took her pale hand into his translucent ones, which used to be so firm and strong, but were now liberally dotted with brown age spots. "Be happy, Becky. It's really all that matters in life. Money and career are okay when you're carving out your place in the world. But you've got Max to think of now. What are you waiting for? Do what your heart says is right, as your mam used to say."

George wasn't aware Rosemary Cottage was hardly habitable or that she'd have no chance of securing a job in Northumberland whilst she was an un-discharged bankrupt and a stuck-off solicitor. But she knew he was right—here in rural Northumberland inventions such as six-minute segments of time-recording, unachievable financial targets, and exorbitant bonus payments seemed obscenely avaricious.

Lapsing into silence, George gently snoozed, worn out from the energy expended on such a lengthy conversation, whilst Rebecca pondered his pep talk. Sipping her tea, her thoughts leapt from guilt, to worry, to shame, and then to panic at her father's failing health. If she was going to take the plunge and move back north, it would have to be soon or it would be too late for her treasured relationship with her father.

The care home manger materialized, a round, bustling, jolly woman in her late fifties, with the sing-song Welsh accent Rebecca loved.

"Hello, Rebecca my dear. How are you?"

"Fine, thanks, Mrs Peters."

"He'll be away 'til lunchtime now. Loves a snooze in that chair in the morning, does your dad. Why don't you come back at two, after lunch? He'll be more refreshed then. He's spending more time sleeping lately. Talks about your mum all the time, though. He adores her, you know, misses her so much."

"Yes, I know," Rebecca said sadly, wishing she had been as lucky in her choice of partner. She rose from the comfort of the flowery, wing-backed chair, reluctant to leave. "See you at two, then, Mrs Peters. I'll bring Max."

"You do that, pet. We all love to see the little livewire."

Rebecca slumped in her car in the Lodge's car park, howling for her miserable choices in life, for the closing days of her father's life, and her own bleak ones ahead. How had she managed to get herself and her beloved family into this mess? How had she dared to inflict such pain on her father and Max? And how could she ever start to put things right?

Wiping away her self-regarding tears, she drew in a deep breath. *Come on, Rebecca. Show some mettle! Do the right thing and sort your life out!*

She determined to do just that!

CHAPTER NINE

"RIGHT! WHERE'S THAT wishes book then?" Deb demanded first thing Monday morning. "Hand it over! I'm holding you to your promise."

Before Rebecca handed *the little green book* to Deb, Nathan glanced at their team manager, Georgina, still engrossed in a complicated call, then scootered his chair to Deb's desk as if keen to get involved.

"The Little Green Book of Wishes." Deb rotated the book in her hand, stroking its emerald cover as though wedding dress silk, parting its pages at the contents page. "'Wishes with your Partner', 'Wishes with Children', or 'Wishes for the World' section? Hey, there's one of your wishes here, Nath, from the 'Wishes with Friends' section—'Real Ale tasting'! Oh, and 'Swishing'! Now that's one I would include on my wish list!"

"I don't understand why you are both so excited." Nathan rolled his eyes. "It's a complete waste of time and energy, if you ask me. Wishes never come true. I'd love to get the supervisor's job when Georgina is promoted to associate next month, but I know I won't, so what's the point applying? Why put myself through all that anxiety and stress? Anyway, it's Becky we're selecting random wishes for, not me. And why put poor Becky through the hassle and potential humiliation of performing challenges from a randomly purchased book extolling the unachievable virtues of fulfilling our deepest desires? Crazy, if you ask me."

He flicked his Baringer & Co pen between his fingers until it became a blur. However, despite his pessimistic forecast, he continued to pour eagerly over the contents section of the little green book with Deb and Rebecca.

"Well, I think it's an excellent idea and so does Fergus. Hey, look, there's even a section on marrying. Thank goodness, 'cos I could do with some seriously helpful tips, we've still got so much to do. I'm up for 'Becoming the Perfect Bride' and 'Maintaining a Successful Marriage'. Might even try 'Co-existing With Your In-laws'." She sniggered.

"Oh, I'm so excited. Look, Becky, 'Amassing a Prestigious Shoe Collection.' Let's study that one and slip off one lunchtime soon to Jimmy Choo's wedding shoe emporium! Come on, what'll be your first challenge from the little green book? You chose the category, but me and Nath are choosing the challenge." She held the book up to Rebecca's face and flicked the pages from back to front, her perfectly plucked, honey-blonde eyebrows disappearing into her fringe.

"Well, I really don't want to go on a date, and my career is rock bottom, so it'll have to be some sort of an activity." Rebecca fervently hoped the selection would be 'Making Maracas' or 'An Afternoon Kite Flying', which she and Max had discovered, but somehow she doubted Deb would let her off so easily.

"Right, now me and Nathan will confer. It'll be a great way of meeting new guys, anyway." She giggled. As she was in love, she expected the whole world to want to be, too. "Mmm, what do you think, Nath?" They huddled together in her cubicle, her blonde mane meeting his dark spikes. "Where will there be lots of hot, single men? Oh, and let's find something she can do with Max, too, this being the first challenge.

"What about 'Taking a Dance Class'? Must be on everyone's wish list that, surely? It suggests the waltz or the tango. Here, did you know the tango is said to have been born in the brothels of Argentina, the dancers connecting chest-to-chest or hip-to-thigh displaying strong and determined passion? What could be better? Only two stars, Becky, must be an easy challenge, right?"

"You're joking. I'm not taking Max to a tango class! Anyway, look what it says at the end. *A dance class such as the tango or the jive is not for the faint-hearted when wishing to meet new people.* No, Deb."

"Well, okay, but I might persuade Fergus to take some lessons with me. We could perform a passionate tango as our first dance at the wedding reception—spice up the night and shock the grannies!"

Her infectious giggle rang around the office, causing Georgina to lift her eyes and throw them a puzzled look. Shaking her short, black curls, she returned to her phone call. It was their lunch break after all.

"Right, 'Exercising Section,' then. What sport have you always had a hankering to try? Yoga? Crossbow shooting? Oh, what about Morris dancing? Is that really a sport?"

"Be serious. I've not done any real exercise since giving birth to Max. Anything too energetic would be the first and last challenge to be attempted from the book and I'd end up in the A&E."

"I suppose that also means 'Climbing Mount Everest' is not going to make Rebecca's wonderful wish list, then?" Deb smirked.

Rebecca's glare said, "Do you think I'm stupid?"

"Right, got it." She held the book up in front of her and Nathan's faces. He glanced at the page and then peered around the cover at Rebecca.

"Sure," Nathan agreed. "As good as any. And Max can join in with that, too, which is what the book is suggesting, I think. There's a great club near us which runs a junior academy and welcomes kids from the age of three."

"What? What are you talking about?" Rebecca's heart hammered against her ribcage, particularly at Nathan's suggestion that Max join her. She had not agreed to involving him in this crazy folly. But her new friends ignored her protestations.

"Yes, I've been to that club with Fergus' nephew. It's great fun. Right, decided." Deb turned the chosen page toward Rebecca. "There you are, Becky, 'Learning to Play Golf'. You can take Max along and have some fun just hitting the balls from the driving range, or there's an American mini golf course to try out. You can enquire about the junior academy whilst you're there for Max. It's an activity you can do together and there'll be lots of men wandering around in that delightful golf gear. You could kill two birds with one golf ball!"

She handed the book to Rebecca, who grabbed it and read out loud, "*Learning to play golf is fun. Hitting a golf ball is easy, but hitting the ball in the direction you want it to go takes an enormous amount of practice.* Mmm. Look at the warning at the end. *Be sure never to stand in close proximity to a golfer's swinging club.* I foresee disaster."

Rebecca shot a glance from Nathan to Deb, disappointed to see not a smidgeon of concession to her dire prediction. And these people were supposed to be her new friends. She grasped her courage 'round the scruff of its neck and drew in a breath.

"Okay, it's as good a start as any. Dad took the game up when he retired. He loved the fresh air, the peace, and tranquility on the course on a crisp spring morning and he'd love to hear me and Max are giving it a go together. We can share golf anecdotes. I accept the challenge, the first 'lucky dip' on Rebecca's Wonderful Wishes Decathlon, but it'll be a couple of weeks before we can go."

She noticed Deb's blue eyes cloud over, and glanced up just in time to slam the book into her desk drawer and affix a smile as Lucinda approached.

"There's a training course scheduled for Saturday, fourth May. I'm asking you all to put the date in your diaries. All excuses denied—three-line whip. It's imperative we stay abreast of the recent developments in family and matrimonial litigation. There've been a number of important Supreme Court decisions in the financial relief field and we need to be fully conversant with the implications of each judgment. The details are on the e-mail Amanda has sent you."

Amanda, Lucinda's secretary, had the highest level of sympathy and respect of the employees of Baringer & Co. She had achieved fifteen years as personal assistant, commencing her servitude before Lucinda had been made partner at the age of twenty nine. She wore the metaphorical skin of a rhino.

Lucinda glanced at the three paralegals staring silently at her, her astute blue eyes resting on the exact spot where they had clustered around the little green book. With a soupcon of malice dancing in her eyes, she turned on her spindly heels and swept from the room in a cloud of cloyingly heavy perfume.

"That's the bank holiday weekend, the witch. I wanted to go up to Edinburgh to see my mam. I'll have to postpone until the Saturday night train which'll be full of inebriated Scots." Still mumbling under his breath, Nathan scooted back to his work

[58]

station, seized his pen, which he set flicking, and replaced his headset.

"I hate her. It was probably her idea for us to do the training on the bank holiday weekend. She's got no friends or family to spend time with, so why should she let us enjoy the break with ours? Me and Fergus had planned on mooching down to his sister's in Brighton for a long weekend. She's getting married next spring, so I'm going to regale her with the benefit of all my research and a bundle of glossy wedding magazines. Fiancées' porn, Fergus calls it! What are you going to do, Becky? Will someone look after Max for you?"

"I'm not sure. I could ask my neighbour, Brian, but as it's a bank holiday he may have plans himself. Oh, what if he can't? I can't miss the training. I need this job and I've got to keep on the right side of Lucinda. She's done so much for me, I don't want to let her down. I'll have to come up with something."

And why did I agree to join a golf session? Max hadn't shown the slightest interest in any sport. *Well, I suppose now he could.*

CHAPTER TEN

REBECCA STEERED INTO Parklands Golf Club's car park. She had booked them a place on the adult and child Try Golf course. Thankfully, the early June weather chose to grace them with the warm caress of a sunny Saturday morning. Driving rain and golf didn't mix, as far as Rebecca was concerned.

As they sauntered to the clubhouse, Rebecca marveled at the blanket of calm and tranquility surrounding the golf course, despite its location in the middle of the city. Even the regularly descending aircraft flights failed to spoil the idyll. The only sounds to reach her ears were the wrens and chaffinches chirping their song—a treat she hadn't paused to notice for years—and the strumming purr of the greenkeeper's industrial-sized grass mower.

She and Max had carefully studied the advice outlined in the little emerald book instead of the required bedtime reading about the exploits of a blue fictional steam locomotive. Giggling, they had pressed the old wooden rolling pin into service to try out their golf club grip. The book had advised that the game could become an obsession, that it'd take years for addicts to lower their handicaps.

Rebecca knew that golf was one obsession she'd never fall into the clutches of and she would certainly not need to be acquainted with the complicated formula for calculating one's golf handicap, realising a degree in mathematics was advisable.

On arrival, Rebecca and Max were directed to the lobby of the driving range to meet the golf pro, and then waited nervously with four other parents and their children who ranged from Max's age to around eight. Most people who play golf were ancient, Rebecca thought. Would the pro be a humourless, middle-aged golf professional who loathed children who couldn't stand still for the full hour's lesson?

"Hi there, everyone. I'm Nikki." A lithe, tanned, mid-twenties girl with a glossy chestnut ponytail tucked into a golf cap sprang forward to greet the anxious group. "Thanks for coming along today to try your hand at golf. It's a fabulous sport, especially as the game lends itself so well to playing as a family. I hope you are all going to have fun as well as learn the basics. We'll start on the mini golf course, just so you can get the feel of the clubs, learn the correct grip and stance. But mainly, to enjoy the game! Okay?"

"Yes, yes, yes." Max bounced, oblivious to the other members of the group, but raising smiles all around.

"Right, adult clubs are over there," Nikki pointed to a white steel basket from which a plethora of golf clubs protruded like over-sized lollipops, "Kid's clubs there. Grab one each and let's go."

As she selected an old dented putter with a pitted grip, Rebecca relaxed. She had not expected a female golf pro when the guy who'd booked her and Max in had said the lessons would be with Nikki Hunter. The young woman's enthusiasm and broad smile decreased the twisting nerves in Rebecca's stomach. Her exuberant personality drew the kids into her wake like the Pied Piper, their miniature golf clubs dragging along behind them, eager to give the sport a chance.

"How old's your little boy?" enquired a tall, slender, nervous-looking parent sporting a candy pink and cream diamond-checkered golf sweater.

"Oh, Max is four."

"I'm Samantha Russell, call me Sam, and this is my son, Ben. He's five. I'm not so sure about playing golf myself, apart from the great jumpers, but Ben is enthusiastic, so we're up for the challenge." She laughed, her blonde, graduated bob falling around her attractive freckled face.

"Same here! I'm Rebecca Mathews, by the way. Call me Becky."

They waited on the side lines surveying Max, Ben, and the three other children who stood obediently in a line in front of Nikki, putters stretched before them.

The group remained silent in concentration as Nikki demonstrated how to grip their clubs, then how to safely swing them like a pendulum as an extension of their arms, adjusting thumbs where required. She ran through the rules, slowly making sure they understood. No club higher than their knees and any child found hitting another with a club would be asked to leave. They nodded, wide-eyed.

"Right then, pick your favourite coloured ball and off you go to hole number one whilst I sort your mums and dads out." And with obedience rarely encountered at home, they trotted off to the first hole.

"We'll let them get on with a couple of holes whilst I demonstrate the grip and swing, then we'll pair back up for a game with score cards." Nikki smiled at the apprehensive expressions on the parents' faces, her slight frame belying her powerful swing and teaching techniques.

Rebecca listened carefully, placing her hands on the putter as instructed, keeping her arms loose but straight, attempting the pendulum action with her shoulders. More nervous giggling and cursing erupted from the adult group than was uttered from the children's, but everyone got the hang of it.

The American-designed, mini-golf course was great fun. Eighteen holes of twists and turns, bridges and mounds, tunnels and water hazards. Laughter regularly erupted, with whooping and cheering as one of the dads scored a hole-in-one. Rebecca's technique was rubbish, her stance too rigid, but she thoroughly enjoyed the new activity. It would be good to share her learning experience with her dad next time they were in Northumberland.

"Same time next week, please." Nikki said. "We'll move on to the driving range, learning the full swing from a tee with a seven iron for those who'd prefer to bring their own clubs. Any questions from today? Well, thank you all for coming, I hope everyone had fun and see you next week." She replaced her pink baseball cap, pulling her chestnut ponytail through the gap at the back, before topping up her glistening apricot lip gloss as she strode off to her next lesson.

"Wow. That was so much fun, Mum. Can we come next week? Nikki is great, isn't she? And I liked Ben, too. He's kind."

"Yes, it was fun, Max, and yes, we'll definitely come back next week."

"Yes, yes, yes." He skipped ahead to the car park.

"Enjoy that?" called one of the dads as he bundled his daughter into the back of his shiny new four-by-four.

"Yes, I did. I think we'll be coming back next week, anyway." She smiled.

"Okay, see you then."

Rebecca fastened Max into his seat. It was the first day in a long time they had had such fun together and Max was buzzing. She'd concentrated so hard on the instructions Nikki was explaining that she'd had no brain space available to wallow in her sad, complicated life. Her spirits lifted, she felt lighter somehow, her forehead less creased, her shoulders less hunched despite her aching elbows.

She'd been fortunate enough to spend her Saturday morning enjoying the fresh air, as the glow of the sunshine drew out her freckles, with her favourite person in the world, experiencing a new sport they both found they loved. She'd had fun. Real fun! And they'd clicked with Sam and her son, Ben. She'd never progress to being allowed onto the golf course, the holes seemed miles away, but she itched to report back to Deb, and Nathan in particular, that as far as the first challenge was concerned, she'd had fun, met new friends and, more importantly, so had Max.

Max's little voice chirped from the back seat. "I'm glad you chose that activity out of your little green wish book, Mummy"

"Me, too, love. Actually, it was Deb from work who chose it for us to try."

"Can we try another one, pleeeease?"

"How about 'Designing, Modelling, and Launching Your Own Kite?'"

"Yes, yes, yes."

CHAPTER ELEVEN

"TOLD YOU SHE'D have fun, Nath. Oh, ye of little faith," said Deb, as Rebecca relayed the details of the third session of the Adult and Child Golf Academy. That week's session had centred on learning how to swing the largest of the golf clubs, the driver.

Deb particularly enjoyed the reluctant report of the embarrassing incident when Rebecca had gritted her teeth so hard as she swung the mammoth club, determined her little white ball of lead would fly at least as far as the fifty yard marker. She'd lost her balance on the upswing and stumbled face first into a pool of water collecting in the ditch at the edge of her bay, producing much hilarity, adult and child, and not enough sympathy from Nikki. But she was having the best time she'd had in years.

The weather had been perfect for June. The golf lessons were providing a welcome diversion from the constant daily struggle Rebecca endured delivering Max to nursery, the slog of the daily commute, maintaining the work rate at Baringer & Co, striving to remain in Lucinda's good books, and leaving her desk in time to rescue Max from nursery before she was charged exorbitant late fees.

Max appeared more relaxed, too. His sleeve-sucking had minimised, so his keyworker had recorded, although not eradicated. He was less concerned about the snide comments made by Stanley, more about what he and his new best friend, Ben, would be learning during the golf activities on Saturday. He was pressing to join the junior academy when the Try Golf sessions finished at the end of July. Rebecca worried she wouldn't be able to afford it, but wasn't prepared to burst his golf ball-shaped bubble quite yet.

"Okay. Next challenge from our sparkling emerald book of wishes," mused Deb.

"Oh, no. Technically, we haven't finished this one yet!"

Ignoring Rebecca's protestations, Deb continued, "I'm afraid it's the 'Wishes with Partners' section this time, my friend. Right, let's start at the beginning. Number one is 'Meeting', which goes hand-in-hand with number two, 'Kissing'." Deb's freckled nose crinkled mischievously in query, her cobalt eyes challenging Rebecca. "Need any help on that score, Becky?"

"Very funny."

"And then number three, 'Romancing'. We'll work through those, and then, if you're successful, we can move on to number four, 'Marrying'."

"I still think this is ridiculous, Deb," Nathan interrupted. "You can't just plan a relationship from suggestions in a wish book. Poor Becky, she's cowering at the very thought, cringing right down to her toes."

"Did she or did she not have a fabulous time at the Try Golf taster sessions? Did she or did she not meet new friends for herself and Max? A complete success, I'd say. Now, shut up or I'll pick one out for you, Nathan. Mmmm, yes, from the 'Partners' section, there's 'Learning to Morris dance'. You can do this one, Nath."

He scowled at her whilst Deb pretended to scan the little gems of wisdom, a flinty look in her determined eyes.

"In this section on procrastination, the book recommends you *enlist the support of friends, start small, and set yourself small-scale deadlines*. Right, Nath, get on with that application to court to see Millie. Rebecca's offered to help you. She's an expert. It's what she did all the time at Harvey & Co and she was frequently successful, weren't you, Becky? Small steps, the book advises. A solicitor's letter initially, I think. Better check with Lucinda first, Becky, make sure she supports Nathan using the firm's letter heading. You can promise to do it in your own time, if needs be."

"Yes, I'll speak to her if you want me to, Nathan. Deb's right, you should take the next step. You haven't seen Millie since Christmas. Nothing'll change until you take formal action."

"I'm taking my own action in my own way. Thank you. But, okay, a letter is a small step in the right direction, just to let Emma know I am determined to maintain a relationship with Millie and will never give up. Can you keep the wording neutral though, Becky? Wouldn't want to inflame the Rugger Boy."

Rebecca was amazed he had agreed. This was a huge step. Had he borrowed the book from her drawer? Had her own challenge success inspired him to move forward? But what did he mean, 'I'm taking my own action?'

"Right, Becky, the date." Deb chewed thoughtfully on the end of her pen before she flicked her eyes to Rebecca's. "Gather up your courage, nothing too formal to start with, just invite someone for a coffee. Is there anyone you've admired from afar? Don't think George Clooney is free!"

"No one at all. Sorry. Boring and dull, I know."

"What about your neighbour, Barry, you sometimes mention? The one who helps out with Max, has a little girl? Sounds ideal."

"It's Brian, and I can't say I've ever admired him from afar, or from close quarters either. But he's a decent enough bloke, good with Max."

"Identity of date solved. Meet-at-café option or picnic-in-the-park option?"

"If it has to be Brian, the picnic-in-the-park option, then we can take Max and Erin."

"On a date? Oh, well, it's your date. Now what to wear and how to ensure you make a good impression. Here's the list, learn them off by heart. You can make notes, too, Nath."

Deb counted them off on her fingers, her long nails painted sparkling emerald green to match her engagement ring.

"*One, dress comfortably. Two, body language is important. Face your date, be interested and receptive, and engage eye contact.* Yes, I get that, you're always slouched over your desk, Becky. Upright, my girl!" And she stuck out her ample breasts. "*Three, comment positively on an item your date is wearing. Four, don't, under any circumstances, moan about ex partners. Five, have fun. Six, don't be afraid to snog his lips off!*" She dissolved into fits of laughter and, disappointingly, so did Nathan.

"That last one was a 'Deb extra', wasn't it?" Rebecca rolled her eyes at her friend.

"What're you three cooking up?" Georgina had concluded one of her marathon calls and wandered over, smiling.

"Becky's off on a date with her neighbour, Brian. We're relying on *The Little Green Book of Wishes'* advice for its success, and then we'll move on to the 'Romancing' and the 'Marrying' sections. It's a real gem! A sparkling emerald in the world of dusty old books.

Next on our agenda is the section on kissing—the dos and the don'ts!"

Eyes stretched wide, Georgina perched her pert, designer-clad bottom on the corner of Rebecca's desk. "I'm interested to hear this."

Rebecca had a lot of respect for Georgina. She hoped that as she progressed up the ranks at Baringer & Co, her sensible, down-to-earth approach would temper the Rottweiler image of the rest of the Baringer & Co partnership—a corporate world where financial targets could be achieved, but also employers were fair to their staff and families.

Georgina towed the partnership line with her dress code. Immaculate navy skirt suit—no trousers allowed for partners—tight-fitting, ice-white cotton shirt, double cuffs linked with cute black cats. Her facial features were sketched with clear charcoal strokes, dark eyebrows, dark eyes and lashes, and deep plum lipstick. With her short black curls pushed neatly behind her ears, she lacked the polished perfection of Lucinda and appeared all the better for it.

"Right here, you read it, Georgina," Deb suggested.

Georgina grabbed the book and crossed her shapely legs, swinging her peep-toe, navy stilettos, and assumed her best advocate's voice. *"Meet his eyes, use open, receptive body language, arms loosely at your side, lean forward, tilting your head so as to avoid bumping noses."*

Deb snorted, placing the back of her left hand to her cheek.

"Your lips gently meet your date's…"

Deb slowly touched her pink frosted lips to her hand.

"Try not to breathe too deeply or too fast."

Deb slurped and sucked at her hand and they all erupted with fits of laughter.

[69]

"And release! Check your date's reaction. If he's horror-struck, then you probably should not repeat!"

More bursts of laughter. All the tension from that morning's hot house of work released, firming their bonds of friendship.

"Look at the next nugget of advice. *If your date's reaction is positive, repeat the process adding a nibble, a soft enticing waft of breath to his earlobe, neck, or hairline.'* That's if he's got any hair, of course!"

Deb was now laughing so hard tears streamed down her rounded pink cheeks. "I've got to pee!" She shot off, clanging the glass door as she dashed to the restrooms, thereby waking the beast.

"What's going on?" Lucinda's face creased into a frown. "Why all the hilarity? No one got any work to do? Georgina?"

"Sorry, Lucinda. Just an article we've read, expelling the pent-up pressure, you know. We're back to the grind now."

Rebecca ducked her head behind her computer and Nathan scooted back to his cubby hole.

"I expect you all to meet your targets at the end of June. If anyone fails to do so, they'll have me to contend with. I'm all for sessions of colleague-bonding, but on your own time, please, not to the detriment of your commitment to Baringer and our clients."

Yeh, right, thought Rebecca. What bonding did Lucinda encourage? But she quashed the disloyal reaction. Lucinda had been her saviour in her darkest hour and she owed her tremendously. If only she would lighten up a little. Didn't she have more in her life than corporate concern? The answer didn't look too promising.

She'd scrutinised her figures for the last quarter and, thankfully, she was on target. But she wanted to prove to Lucinda that she could work even harder, exceed that expectation and she had a week to do it. Not only did she need her job, but she wanted to make progress toward revitalising her career prospects and resuming her position on the solicitors' roll.

Deb returned, refusing to be deflected from her march along the road toward the cure of Rebecca's list addiction and to stumble upon love on the way. "So, when's the date going to be? I say a week on Saturday, sixth July?"

CHAPTER TWELVE

SATURDAY, SIXTH JULY, was a day Rebecca had been dreading. Not the best frame of mind to be in for a date. She had only caved in and agreed to it under threat of excommunication from Deb and Nathan.

It was only a picnic in the park with Brian, Erin, and Max, an activity they'd had fun doing last summer when the sun wore its sombrero. But because Deb and Nathan had crafted the innocent outing into the beginnings of the romance of the decade, her stomach screamed nerves and nausea.

On paper, Brian Thomas Garside's attributes appeared ideal. Any random guy sounded ideal to Deb, caught up in her whirlwind of taffeta and roses. Maybe she should date an axe murderer? Deb wouldn't care as long as he fulfilled the marriage criteria.

A single father, Brian's ex-partner had returned to her native Australia when Erin turned eighteen months old, only visiting her daughter once since her abandonment.

Erin was a sweet, calm child, blonde hair frothing like bubbles around her chubby face. Like Max, Erin had recently celebrated her fourth birthday and they would be attending the same school when they started in September.

Rebecca didn't dislike Brian by any means. He'd proved to be a caring friend, ally, and occasional babysitter. He was a dab hand at small DIY projects and an all-around decent person. Max liked him, too, another plus point for Brian. Yes, on her inevitable list of Brian's Pros and Cons, theory had it that he scored highly on the Pros.

"We're off to the park with Brian and Erin this morning, taking a picnic for lunch, Max. Why don't you find your red Frisbee and you and Erin can have some fun chasing it?"

"Yes, yes, yes!" Max bounced off to locate it in the jungle of plastic monstrosities in his chaotic bedroom.

After she assembled the finishing touches to the picnic, Rebecca squeezed a chilled bottle of Rosado Cava into the wicker basket, allegedly selected after careful consideration of the advice given in the little green book, but mainly because it had been on special offer at the deli on the corner of her street.

Together she, Deb, and Nathan had scoured and scrutinised the pages of wisdom on 'Romancing'. Deb had even flicked ahead to 'Marrying'. Very funny! It had only served to produce even more needless anxiety for a jittery Rebecca.

A gentle rap on her door announced Brian and Erin's arrival.

"Hi. Are we early?"

"No, just liberating the picnic blanket from hibernation under the stairs. All the food's prepared over in that wicker basket. Max is very excited and aren't we lucky with the weather?" she gushed. Why was the pretext of the picnic having such an unfavourable effect on what was essentially an outing they had undertaken

[73]

several times successfully in the past? "Maybe they can dig in the sand pit or splash in the paddling pool after lunch."

"Well, we'll see. I don't usually allow Erin to play in dirty water. You just can't be sure what deadly viruses are floating around in those public paddling pools. Don't want to take the risk."

"No. Well. Come on, Max. Off we go!"

Max and Erin cantered ahead, delighted to be released from the enclosed space of the apartment, stretching their legs, happy in each other's company. Max's spiky hair brushing Erin's blonde cloud of ringlets as they bobbed along holding hands was a photographer's dream snapshot.

Curiously tongue-tied, Rebecca's mouth was as dry as dust, her mind blank of all interesting anecdotes or any of the advice revised with Deb and Nathan from the little green book.

"How's your week been?" Good grief, how boring was she?

"Oh, exhausting of course. My IT job really saps the energy out of your bones, and I don't have to tell you how draining it is caring for a young child on your own. But it's a great idea to step out of the monotony for a picnic in the park—very generous of you to provide the food, Rebecca. Erin is so excited it was a struggle to settle her down last night."

"Oh, the food was no trouble. Thanks for coming along. And I must say thanks again for having Max for me on the bank holiday. He adored the trip to the cinema. We rarely get the chance to go. He's still chattering about Lightening McQueen and Mater and Holly Shiftwell!"

Silence again. Brian smiled shyly at her. Unfortunately, his soft chestnut eyes and gentle expression were not enough for Rebecca to overlook one of her pet hates—Brian sported a mousey brown beard. Not one of those fashionable, sexy, Gary Barlow, bit-more-than-a-five-o'clock-shadow types. No, his was a full face mat with a slight curl in it!

She fleetingly thought back to the office hilarity at the 'Kissing' section in the little green book and, glancing out of the corner of her eye at Brian's beard, she experienced a wave of revulsion. No way would she even come close to dragging up that piece of advice today. But he was a genuinely decent guy, so she'd give him a chance.

Ravenscourt Park was already alive with noisy families. Small children released from the tedium of the school timetable scampered freely—the warm sunshine thawing any threat of tantrums—playing ball games, shrieking, and splashing in the germ-ridden pool. Rebecca shook out the red tartan blanket and Max and Erin ran off with the Frisbee.

Rebecca extended her pale legs out in front of her, leaning on her outstretched arms, glad she'd chosen her new denim shorts, relieved she'd remembered to shave the fuzz from her long slender legs. She turned her face up to the warming sun for once not caring about her emerging freckles.

Surreptitiously peeking from beneath her lowered lids, Rebecca scanned Brian's long legs encased in thick brown cords, her eyes travelling down to his open-toe brown leather sandals worn without socks. His toenails screamed out for one of Deb's pedicures. She quickly averted her gaze.

Good heavens, if this wasn't supposed to be a pseudo-date, she wouldn't have noticed any of these physical imperfections. She'd known Brian for two years as her neighbour and occasional babysitter and she'd never before bothered to consider his attributes, negative or positive. What a shallow person she was!

"Come on, kids. Let's devour the picnic." Rebecca called to Max and Erin, unable to meet Brian's confused expression or to dredge up any more scintillating conversation.

"Yes, yes, yes," they sang in unison.

Rebecca unpacked the wicker basket and handed Brian the Cava to open. A shot of cool, bubbly elixir would provide the thaw their 'date' needed.

"Very generous of you, Rebecca, this all looks lovely, but I'll decline the alcohol if you don't mind. I never indulge when Erin's around."

Rebecca felt like a reckless, alcoholic parent, intent on getting plastered and staggering back to her tiny flat in an intoxicated stupor, dragging her bedraggled child in the wake of her alcohol fumes.

"Well, I thought one of these plastic flutes with our food would be okay. Just for today. No work tomorrow, you know?"

"I won't, but thanks anyway."

Rebecca busied herself laying out miniature bagels filled with cream cheese and smoked salmon, roast beef and ham sandwiches with their crusts cut off, and large plastic containers of Waldorf salad and spicy Moroccan couscous.

"Strawberries and cream for dessert!"

"Oh, Rebecca, sorry. Erin and I are vegan now. We'll just have the couscous and salad, which I must say look delicious."

Rebecca and Deb had spent their whole lunch hour yesterday shopping in the upmarket Italian Deli around the corner from their office for the ingredients for the picnic-cum-date, and Rebecca had devoted all morning to assembling the perfect picnic. Unfortunately, veganism had not featured in either hers or Deb's deliberations.

"Oh, I'm so sorry, Brian. I never thought to ask you your food preferences. How rude of me to assume."

Max wolfed down two ham sandwiches, anxious to return to his Frisbee game. Rebecca caught an envious look from Erin as she tucked into a plate of watercress and couscous. She experienced an unaccountable stab of guilt as she relished how well the sparkling rose went with smoked salmon and sunshine.

"Can we go and splash in the paddling pool, Mum?"

"Yes, love. Have fun!" Rebecca said, and then remembered Brian's dire warning of the water swarming with a concoction of diseases. "Oh, erm, that's if Erin's dad is okay with that, Max."

"Well, Erin, I'd rather you didn't, you know. Remember what Daddy told you about the extensive range of germs inhabiting dirty water. I don't want you to get sick."

"No, Daddy." Her face fell forlorn and Rebecca's heart flipped over in sympathy at the veritable lack of joy allowed in the little girl's life.

She scrambled to her feet. "Let's all play Frisbee," she declared, over-jolly.

They passed a pleasant hour zooming the Frisbee between the four of them, then decided to make their way home when Brian announced the weather forecast had promised rain—not a cloud in the sky—and Rebecca agreed gratefully.

"Thanks, Rebecca. Erin and I had fun today. We'll do the picnic next time, eh?"

Not likely, thought Rebecca and immediately cursed herself and Deb, for not expanding on the date scenario in the direction of how one politely refused a second date, instead of the scenario Deb preferred, to concentrate on of how to get your date to ask you to marry him!

"Yes, that would be lovely," she said, as she bundled Max through her chipped, moss-green front door for fear Brian would 'approach her with positive body language, direct eye contact, and his beard tilted toward her.'

It was her fault, she reasoned. She could raise no enthusiasm or passion for anyone. She'd experienced no spark of romantic interest, in fact if she were bluntly honest, she'd been repelled by his no-alcohol, no-meat, no-splashing, no-fun agenda.

She'd never felt repulsed when dating Bradley, despite his exhibiting some rather unusual personal hygiene traits. Was she still subconsciously in love with him? His immaculate grooming, intoxicating cloud of aftershave, crisp cotton designer-label shirts and linen trousers, his toned, tanned body? Had she succumbed to the human frailty of only pursuing those who'd hurt her the most?

Well, at least she had performed her part of her deal with Deb the Date Maker. No more dates! The item on her wish list that had been a fixture for so long—the happy family scenario for her and Max—was unachievable.

CHAPTER THIRTEEN

"I'M SO DISAPPOINTED. Did you give it your best shot? Did you adopt the positive body language, direct eye contact, and smile? Then I just can't understand it!" Deb took Rebecca's failed date as a personal insult.

"Exactly what I told you," Nathan said. "You can't manufacture a successful date. She's got to at least fancy the guy, the juices of passion have to flow. He sounds mind-numbingly dull to me—inevitable if he works in IT!"

Deb and Nathan had been ping-ponging arguments for the last twenty minutes completely ignoring Rebecca. Every conversation, every word exchanged on her 'date' had been relayed by Rebecca under stiff cross-examination and was now being dissected, every glance, every nuance disclosed was considered for its evidence of a blossoming relationship.

"Oh, well, we can't all be as lucky as me and Fergus," Deb relented at last. "We had coffee and chocolate fudge cake with

Reverend Briggs on Saturday afternoon. He's happy to allow us to recite our own poems to each other during our vows. The chapel is wedding picture-book perfect. Our photos will be stunning. Only four months to go but there's still so much to organise.

"I'm insisting on accompanying Mum and her best friend, Margaret, to town next weekend to select her outfit and hat. I'm thinking pale lilac or lavender, complimenting the Royal purple theme, but she's settled on insipid lemon. The colour really drains one's complexion, I think, so I'm going with her to arbitrate. Right," Deb said, suddenly turning her search beam on Rebecca, who'd mistakenly assumed she had avoided any further interrogation. "Chalk that date up to experience. Next challenge!"

"Oh, Deb, can't we call it a day? The picnic wasn't a huge success because I knew it was supposed to be a date and that piled the pressure on. I wasn't my usual relaxed self." Rebecca pulled a face. When was she ever relaxed? "And I only noticed Brian's quirkiness because I was looking for an excuse not to take things further. And what better excuse than his manky feet? Yak!"

"Okay, not a date, but another activity. You and Max took great pleasure in playing golf together. A real success, wouldn't you agree? What about a challenge from the 'Wishes for Friends' section this time—no Max? Me and Fergus will babysit. I'm planning on four, maybe five children, so the more experience Fergus has with kids the better he will be prepared. What have you always enjoyed doing? Is there a hobby or latent talent you had before the legal profession inserted its evil claws into your soft, milky-white skin?"

"Oh, I don't know, Deb. I should be spending my spare time with Max. It's the summer holidays soon. I need to return to Northumberland to visit Dad and to chase that useless Henry of an estate agent again. I get farmed off to the receptionist whenever I telephone from London, so I need to visit him face to face, see the

[80]

whites of his eyes, as Dad always advises. I'm considering changing agents or going dual. The summer months are the best time to press the many attributes of the cottage. That's when the place is heaving with holiday makers, ramblers, cyclists, and hikers walking the length of Hadrian's Wall, maybe searching for a pretty little cottage as a holiday home. I can't chance missing the summer season or it'll be another six months languishing on the stagnant housing market!"

"What's Mr Estate Agent like? Is he a contender?"

"Stop it, Deb. But actually, yes, he is handsome, in a Hooray Henry sort of way—crisp pink shirt, braces, glint of gold cufflinks, drives the obligatory black, four-wheel-drive tank with tinted windows. But all I desire from him is a sale. He sold the cottage to me in the first place, spun the fairy tale that there were prospective purchasers queuing up to buy it, advising I should put in an offer quick or lose it. Not sure that was true if the last twelve months are anything to go by, but he had me at 'Ivory Roses climbing around the heavy oak front door.' I'd love to have a free reign and unlimited budget to throw at the interior design."

Rebecca affected a creative director stance, throwing one elegant hand expressively wide, lodging the other firmly on her hip. "Darlings, I see modern farmhouse chintz, celestial blue and winter teal with a splash of crushed peppermint in the lounge. Over here we encounter a huge indispensable cream-coloured solid fuel Aga, so I'm thinking roasted pumpkin on the chimney breast wall, Californian sands on the window wall to reflect the buttercups of the adjacent field. Moving up to the master bedroom, I recommend feminine and girly, none of that minimalist beige and taupe Bradley insisted on, so it will be dressed in candy pink, toned down with water lily and pale rose."

She giggled and continued. "Master Max Bradley Mathews, I'm sure, will demand Thomas blue, with accents of Percy green. Hey"—she resumed her seat in her swivel chair at her desk—"did you know there's a specialist stencil library which supplies the whole country with every stencil imaginable, just along the road from Rosemary Cottage, in Stocksfield? You should see it. We visited to explore the library and the attached manor house—every single room, including the bathroom, which was my favourite, had been lovingly and meticulously stencilled—on a 'school trip' during an adult education course I joined when I was reading for my law degree at Durham. Interior design is the path I always wanted to pursue, before the law elbowed my creative ambitions sideways."

"That's it then," Deb exclaimed, her eyes shining. "I happen to know there's an interior design taster course offered at our local college this Saturday. That's where I'm spending my Wednesday nights, learning the intricate art of sugarcraft, designing elaborate posies, delicate leaves, and berries for my wedding cake decoration. Drop Max 'round at ours on Saturday morning and we can spend the day up to our eyes in jams, cream, and icing sugar for cupcakes. It's our homework this week!" She giggled.

"Mum, and me, and my auntie, Jennifer, are performing a trial run for the fruit wedding cakes, too. Max'll love it. He can make as much mess as he likes, and you can go off to college for a day of creative therapy. Try it out, take some 'me time' for your own sanity, Becky. When's the last time you did anything which wasn't connected with work or Max?"

"That's a ridiculous suggestion, Deb," Nathan butted in. "If she's got a free day with a babysitter, she should be doing the 'Divorce and Beyond' training seminar Lucinda wants us to do, not indulge in our 'creative hobbies.' I've been roped into attending on

[82]

Saturday morning, and then I'm straight off to my meeting afterwards."

"What meeting's that, Nathan?" Deb enquired, her eyes boring into Nathan's.

"Oh, erm, I meant meeting the lads down the Fox & Hounds for a few drinks. Saturday night, you know."

Deb narrowed her eyes suspiciously. "That isn't what you meant. You're not a closet alcoholic, are you? Or attending Comic Book Fans Anonymous? No? A weird wizard's Magical Self-Help Group for Miserable Magicians?"

"Funny girl, Deb."

"Mmm. Any news from Emma's solicitors yet? After the letter Becky sent?"

"Actually, yes. Emma's thinking carefully about her plans for the summer holidays whilst Millie is off school. I'm hopeful she might agree to allow her to spend a few days with me in Edinburgh. Mam's oncologist warned us her cancer is becoming more aggressive and she's had all the chemo she can manage for the time being. Her heart's weakened, so they have to be careful. I'm really pinning my hopes on these holidays. It's probably the last chance for Mam to see Millie."

"Oh, Nathan, I hope Emma realises it's the right thing to do. We did mention court proceedings in the letter, but it'll take months before a final decision is made by the Family Proceedings Court after the welfare reports have been prepared," Rebecca said.

Rebecca had a huge amount of sympathy for Nathan's predicament. His options were sparse, the timescales out of his control. Perhaps the meeting he hadn't wanted to expand on *was* a self-help or support group to guide him through this difficult time. He did seem more assertive.

"WELL, DID YOU have fun?" Rebecca knew the answer straightaway.

Max was covered in a light dusting of flour and splodges of red icing, at least that's what she hoped it was! He pouted ruby red lipstick, a la Marilyn Munro! His green eyes were wide and bright, his pupils dilated—a sugar rush!

"Yes, yes, yes."

"How many cupcakes have you made?" The little buns were piled in high, tumbling pyramids on every available surface.

"Seventy two, and we've iced them all, haven't we, chum?" said Fergus. "Some more professional than others, I have to admit. Deb's decorated those with the cute daisies, mine are these with the tiny marshmallows and little chocolate balls, and those lurid green and black ones are Max's. Great job, buddy, high five." The sugar high was not confined to Max!

The kitchen of the Bell family home was a scene from a kitchen nightmare. Deb had not graduated from the culinary school of thought which preached bakers should tidy up as they went along. Every available surface was strewn with brightly decorated mixing bowls, spatulas caked in icing, pastel-coloured paper cases, and in pride of place in the centre of their huge pine table rose a deep, circular fruit cake on a pedestal. The aroma was an elixir to the nostrils. Lemon-coloured icing drizzled down the sides of the fruit cake, sliding the tiny white daisies in its lava flow.

She glanced through the open back door into the garden beyond, where on the green, wooden patio decking the table was bedecked with a yellow gingham table cloth, bright sunshine-yellow plastic plates and cups, and a tower of homemade fruit scones, accompanied by homemade raspberry jam in a glass dish with buttery-yellow clotted cream.

"Hey, Becky! It's been an awesome day." Deb smiled when she caught sight of her friend. "Fergus and Max are demon bakers. I'm not sure now whether I'll be icing my own wedding cake, though. Might get the fruit cakes we've made from Gran's secret recipe professionally iced. How did you get on? Are your creative juices flowing like the icing on my experimental wedding cake?"

"I've had the most fantastic day. Thank you so much for entertaining Max. Yes, such as I possess it, the artistic flair came flooding back. We learned about colour wheels, mood boards, textures, printing, stenciling. The best fun of all was using the glue gun—a gadget that's definitely going on my Christmas wish list! Oh, if I'm even allowed to have a Christmas wish list. Here, I made this for you."

She presented Deb with a handmade, brown paper carrier bag with woven string handles, printed with bells and Deb and Fergus' entwined names.

"In our next session we're designing and producing a stained-glass panel, using lead and a soldering iron. If you agree, I'd love to design a stained-glass piece for your wedding present, intertwined names similar to the design on the bag, wedding rings, hearts, bells. What's your surname going to be when you're married?"

"Horne. Deborah Marie Horne," Deb said proudly.

"You're going from a Bell to a Horne?"

"Yep."

"Made for each other, you two are!" Rebecca laughed. In that moment, Rebecca realized that over the last three months since she'd had the good fortune to meet Deb, she had never laughed or smiled so much in years. She'd assumed working in an open-office environment would be distracting, that she would resent not having her own private sanctuary to prepare her complex legal cases, but the complete opposite had transpired. She only had to lean to the left or right for a word of support, the answer to a difficult query, or the suggestion of a cappuccino. She had a lot to give thanks to her friend and colleague for, apart from her ban on drawing up her beloved lists. Without them, Rebecca still felt adrift, with no structure or control in her life.

"Thanks, Becky, that's a kind and intimately personal gift. We'd be honoured to give it pride of place in our new home. I'm delighted you enjoyed your day-off-duty so much," she said softly, squeezing her tightly. "A little bit of self-indulgence stretches a long way, even though me and Ferg seem to be the beneficiaries of your day's toil."

"I was so totally immersed in the projects—crafting with my fingers and a different part of my brain—that I'm ashamed to admit I wasn't permanently anxious or frazzled wondering what Max was up to, whether he was happy and safe. I'd love to pursue a career in interior design. Maybe I will, one fine day."

CHAPTER FOURTEEN

"COME ON, MAX darling, pull those trainers on. It's the perfect day for flying kites."

"Yes, yes, yes!"

The previous evening, as they snuggled up enveloped in Max's voluminous duvet winding down to sleep, they'd embroidered the stories of their respective day's activities for each other's giggling enjoyment, happy to be back together. They'd made a pact that tomorrow—Sunday—they would select a joint activity.

Rebecca had delved into the little green book for its inspiration, but Max reminded her that the rainbow-coloured kite they had purchased as a lazy alternative to the 'make it yourself' project—unable to accompany them on the picnic with Brian and Erin due to the fickle weather and teeming crowds—still languished in the cupboard under the stairs. She had checked the weather forecast for the following day and to their delight a light breeze was predicted.

Instead of the usual bedtime foray into the trainspotting world of Thomas, Percy, Henry, and Gordon, they scrutinised the pearls of wisdom cultivated from the pages of the emerald tome, paying close attention to the safety advice. 'No flying close to trees or power lines—that can be dangerous. No running with the kite—you could trip or bump into people. Hold the wooden spool firmly to avoid string burn.'

They drifted off to sleep, Max's soft, warm body spooned against Rebecca, each relishing the proximity of the most adored person in their lives.

ON THAT EARLY Sunday morning in July, the park was deserted, save for the hardy dog walkers and the odd obsessive jogger, due to the increasing breeze which Rebecca would have described as a moderate wind. She prayed flying a kite wouldn't require too much strength or talent, as she possessed neither.

Nevertheless, she extracted the brightly coloured, diamond-shaped kite from its excess of packaging. Max's deft little fingers straightened out its beribboned tail on the grassy slope. The kite tail was not, as Rebecca had assumed, purely for aesthetics. It served to drag out the kite's base and keep its nose high in the air, increasing its stability.

"Right, Max, remember what we read last night? Backs to the oncoming wind, which I think is this way." She positioned Max's back into her stomach, reaching down over his skinny shoulders, placing her hands over his on the wooden bobbin of twine. The kite lay motionless on the grass in front of them.

"How does it fly into the sky, Mum?"

"Not sure, Max. You stand as still as you can and hold on as tight as you can. I'll lift the kite into the air, see if that does the trick."

She knelt down, her flying amber hair spreading wide into the increasing breeze, producing the impression of an electrocuted Titian temptress. Raising the kite to her full five-foot-eight-plus arm's length and tiptoes and, for good measure, adding a jump, Rebecca launched the reluctant paper bird skyward. It promptly nose-dived back to the ground, flat as a pancake.

Their eyes met, green on green, and they giggled.

"My turn, Mum," said Max, transferring the wooden spool to Rebecca's outstretched hands. He retrieved the kite, dropped a kiss on its face, and copied Rebecca's volleyball leap, producing the same disappointing result.

"Hi! Having trouble?" a man with an antipodean twang enquired.

"Hi! Yes, you could say that. Our kite prefers terra firma to the freedom of the skies, it seems," Rebecca replied, smiling at the handsome Australian guy, knitted hat pulled over his ears, accompanied by his attractive Dalmatian puppy. Max slunk behind her, his coat sleeve firmly gripped between his teeth.

"Would you like me to get you started? The launch is the most difficult part and there *is* a knack to it, but once the kite's up there in the sky it's an exhilarating experience, I can assure you!"

Rebecca glanced at Max, weighing the desire for the morning's kite-flying expedition not to be a total disaster against the fact she'd have to take responsibility for the Dalmatian's lead during take-off which would traumatise Max.

The Australian saw her hesitation and backed off. "No worries." He held up his hand. "I could be any old scuddy dog

[89]

walker." He flashed his perfectly straight, intensely white teeth in a friendly smile.

"Oh, no, it's just my son has a phobia of dogs, well, any four-legged animal. I was just thinking through the technicalities of accepting your kind offer."

"It'll only take a second to get this tiddler up to the heavens. Here." He shoved the red leather lead into Rebecca's hand and grabbed the spool, his long-legged strides launching him half way down the hill in no time. His dog plonked down his bottom, docile, regarding him with interest, head tipped to one side, unconcerned at being abandoned in the care of strangers.

Amazingly, the kite leapt high into the air, prancing like a sky nymph, and Max, forgetting the proximity of the Dalmatian, pogoed in delight.

"Yes, yes, yes."

The Australian Samaritan stomped back up the hill, keeping the tether taut, as the kite ducked and dived, performing an animated aerial dance for its enthralled audience. He handed the spool to Rebecca, showing her how to handle the line like a horse's harness. She snuggled Max's back into her stomach, allowing him to take the reins under her supervision.

"Thanks."

"No worries. It's a fun activity. Flown kites since I was a kid in Adelaide. Not done it for a while, but maybe I'll unearth my fighter kite. Hand painted it myself!" He stuck out his huge hand, "Scott Barker, at your service. And this is my faithful canine companion, Suzie."

"Oh." She tentatively removed one hand from the straining bobbin to be grasped in a powerful shake. "Rebecca and Max."

"You know, kites can teach kids all sorts of useful stuff. There's the science and physics side—kite flying can introduce kids to aerodynamics, witnessing the enthralling spectacle of the wind catching the underside of the kite's wing causing it to lift gracefully into the air.

"There's the history and culture side, too. Kites can be traced back at least two thousand years to the Chinese who not only flew them for pleasure and sport, but they displayed elaborately crafted, red and gold kites during cultural festivals."

Scott's freckled face became animated as he leapt forward to grab the spool, bringing their errant kite back under control.

"Then there's the technology side—kite-building is fascinating. It's not just glue and sticks, you know. The first designs were made with bamboo and fine silk thread, with bamboo pieces fashioned into tiny whistles making the kites musical as they cavorted through the sky.

"Then there's my favourite, the sport of kite-fighting! In China and the Far East it's a really big deal. There're even events and exhibitions in Australia now. Did you know that a fighting kite's string is strengthened and sharpened so it can slash the rival's kite on impact? Some fliers even use ground glass glued onto fishing twine. Don't agree with that myself. In a duel, the loser forfeits his kite—the winner takes all!

"And finally, there's also the meteorological side—checking the weather conditions on the morning of a competition. You can check, too, Max, look how the leaves on the trees are blowing and leaning. Look at the Union flag on the building over there. Notice which way it flaps in the wind?" Scott stood back. "Sorry, probably boring you senseless!"

"Are you joking?" Rebecca pointed to Max, who stood transfixed, gawping at Scott. He accepted this observation as permission to show off and, handing Susie's lead to Rebecca again, he grabbed the spool, treating them and an assembled audience of

[91]

dog walkers and morning joggers to a kite display of swooping, plunging elegance—a true 'free spirit of the skies.'

After a particularly spectacular lunge producing a round of applause, the kite kamakasied, nose first, onto the grassy slope. Max sprang off to collect it, whilst Scott frantically wound in the string, handing the spool over to Max as they came together.

"Awesome!" they shouted in unison and high-fived. The audience dissipated, continuing their solitary meanders.

Scott turned to Rebecca as she tried to calm her medusa-style hair in the mounting wind. "Fancy a coffee sometime, Rebecca? I promise not to mention kites, although I may mention wind-surfing. It's my other passion!"

Something about the way he pronounced her name in his Australian drawl made it sound sensual, and a murmuring of desire stirred within Rebecca's presumed frozen loins. She enjoyed the long-forgotten sensation.

"I'd love that." She met his eyes as he whipped off his beanie hat and the sexual jolt zapped her again. He was exactly as she imagined the archetypal Aussie surfer to be. Strong, firm physique, sun-streaked, tousled curls sprang back to life once released from their containment, fringe falling into his brilliant blue eyes. If there was a polar opposite to the clean smooth lines of Bradley, mirror in his front pocket, comb in the back, he had materialised in front of her, scrabbling in his black jeans pocket for a scrap of paper to scribble his mobile number on.

"Give me a bell. Coffee or an afternoon flying, your call. Bye, Max buddy!" He fist bumped Max then jogged off, Susie lolloping at his side.

The wind, now bordering on gale force in Rebecca's view, was clearing the park of visitors. So, experiencing a warm glow in the region of her lower stomach, Rebecca and Max leant in and battled their way home, the newly-respected rainbow kite tucked firmly under Rebecca's arm.

"That was awesome fun, Mum. Scott was great. *Your Little Green Book of Fun* is the best book ever. I love it! What can we do next? Don't forget you promised making play dough and whatever maracas are, but what else is in there, Mum?"

Max was right. The book's myriad suggestions had ensured they escaped from the confines of their poky flat and experienced activities they otherwise would never have encountered and met people they would never have met. It was the best ten pounds Rebecca had ever spent. She was even coming 'round to the idea that an *ad hoc* 'dip in, dip out' attitude to life was an adventure in itself—although she wasn't cured of her list addiction just yet.

Now even Max was enthusiastically singing the book's virtues. Between Deb, Nathan, Georgina, and Max, she would have every challenge completed by Christmas! Well, perhaps not the 'Marrying' or the 'Co-existing with your in-laws'. Although with her newly dilated self-esteem…

CHAPTER FIFTEEN

"PLEASE, BRADLEY, IT'S the summer holidays." Rebecca realised a pleading note had entered her voice. Despite knowing her tone would annoy Bradley, she couldn't help her desperation for Max to spend time with his father creep into every conversation she had with him. "Max would love to escape for a few hours outside in the sunshine instead of being stuck in Tumble Teds all day. Or you could take him somewhere during the weekend, so you don't have to lose any time at work. He'd love to see you and Cheryl."

Rebecca had only met Cheryl once—a willowy, ebony-haired, perfectly groomed, immaculate match for Bradley. The jury was out on Max spending time with someone he'd view as a stranger, but if it meant he could spend some time with his father, she was prepared to set her own reservations aside.

"Rebecca, you know I can't just bunk off an afternoon from work. That's a ridiculously naïve suggestion. I'm so frazzled with the complexities of the Glastonburg deal, but it'll complete in three or four weeks and I might be able to find a window in my schedule then. I'll need to check it out with Cheryl, too. She's not a children-person, though—one of the things I love about her."

What's a children-person, thought Rebecca.

"Anyway, I'm sick of you pushing Max onto me. It was your crazy decision to have a child. You were under no illusions as to my take on that failure in your judgment. My career has to take priority, Rebecca. I'm climbing the corporate ladder even if you've slipped off it, and I don't need any distractions. The Glastonburg deal has to run smoothly and, if it does, I'm hoping John Farringdon will notice my commitment and expertise. If I'm off gallivanting with a four year old and an issue crops up on the case, what then?"

"He's your *son*, Bradley. Not some random child from the local foster home! He's sweet, mischievous, full of energy and enthusiasm, with only a mild addiction to all things pertaining to locomotives and steam engines and despite what you think, you would really enjoy his company. He needs to have a relationship with you."

"A snotty four year old? What would we do that I would find even the remotest bit interesting? Cheryl and I are off to Radley Hall for a couples' spa treatment next weekend and then we're having a few days jaunt to Paris at the end of August shopping for the Bali trip. Would a four year old fit into this lifestyle? I don't think so!"

"I need to visit Dad during the summer holidays. I've got a week's leave toward the end of August, but if you'd take Max one Saturday it means I could shoot up before the end of July, too. He's very frail, Brad, and Max struggles with the frequent long journeys."

"Sorry, Rebecca, no can do, not until the Glastonburg deal is laid to bed."

She took a deep calming breath, preparing to ask the next question. She had no funds to arrange any activities for Max over the summer months and he had his heart set on the Junior Golf Academy with Ben.

"Is there any chance you can find fifty pounds for Max to attend Junior Golf Academy in August? He's enjoyed attending it so much so far and met another boy who he gets on well with. I can't find the money, which means he won't be able to attend unless you can help out. Please, Bradley, for Max."

"Look, Rebecca, are you deaf? You've just heard me explain to you what my commitments are for the next few weeks and I've got Bali coming up. I'll have no spare cash myself. Don't lay the guilt on me. You decided on the family scenario, not me. Why should my lifestyle suffer because of your selfish choices? Children are expensive items—you should have factored that in to the equation before deciding to produce one.

"And whilst we are on the subject of questionable choices, I'm embarrassed about your position with Baringer & Co. John Farringdon delayed me in the director's corridor yesterday to interrogate me on whether it was correct you had been struck off the solicitors' roll and were now working as a paralegal at Baringer. I was mortified. How can you put me in this position? Couldn't you have taken a job outside the legal profession, kept a low profile for my sake? Oh no, you have the audacity to flaunt your failures in my face.

"And what's happening with that white elephant in the sticks? Why hasn't it sold yet? It's been languishing on the market for nearly a year now. The sooner you get rid of it and pay back your debts, the sooner you'll be able to discharge your bankruptcy and get on with a decent career, one which pays better so you're not always asking me for money. It's laughable you being employed as a paralegal when you graduated with a first class honours degree from Durham.

"And those colleagues you are associating with. That fantasy fanatic, Nathan Atkins, is crazy. I overheard one of our secretaries gossiping about him the other day. I hope you aren't allowing him anywhere near Max."

"Whom I choose to associate with is none of your business and as you refuse to have any contact with your son, Bradley, I fail to see how you can dictate any rules about who he has contact with. Nathan is a decent guy, but you wouldn't recognise decency if it slapped you in your clean-shaven, perfume-doused face.

"I'm upset and disappointed Max will not be able to attend his longed-for Golf Academy, but we'll work something out. Enjoy Paris, the couples' spa, and Bali." She slammed the phone down before her strangled voice cracked.

Rebecca shielded Max from his father's disinterest as much as she was able, but as he had not laid eyes on him since Christmas, Max had stopped asking about him anyway. She was saddened more than anything for Max's lost opportunity to spend time with his father, to build up the same solid relationship she'd enjoyed with hers. She couldn't replicate this for Max. He needed, and deserved, two parents who loved him and placed him at the centre of their universe. She strove hard to be the best parent she could, but she knew she fell woefully short.

But she worried most about what effect this indifference would have on Max as he grew older, old enough to realise his father's coolness and apathy, his rejection of the role of father. She could barricade him with protective walls as high as the sky, but it would store up angst for Max's future adulthood and Rebecca was powerless to change anything. No amount of carefully researched lists would serve to produce a solution to this conundrum.

The situation was all the more surprising to her knowing Bradley had had a difficult relationship with his own father, who had left his mother when Bradley and his brother, Adam, were seven and five. She had foolishly believed that traumatic event would have spurred Bradley on to determine to be a better father himself, knowing how the neglect had seared pain through his heart during his teenage years. But, sadly for Max, his father's past had had the opposite effect.

She panicked Max would grow up to have the same attitude as his father and was adamant she would strive to provide Max with a settled, caring family life as soon as she was able. But that dream had dwindled to naught. It was so difficult to meet new people, new potential partners. The 'happy family' dream languished at the bottom of her bucket list as the least likely to be achieved.

She thought back to the disastrous 'date' with Brian and shuddered at the anticipation of having to endure numerous similar scenarios. But it was the only way forward if she wanted to even step down the path to the goal she had set for her and Max's futures. She'd grit her teeth and instead of the item screaming failure from the doldrums of her bucket list, she'd switch to her new tactic and rely on the little green book of random miracles.

More immediately, she'd have to break the news to Max that there would only be a week's reprieve from nursery, when they would spend time together in Northumberland. She had requested an additional week's leave, but Lucinda had refused, glaring at her as though she had crawled from under a scummy stone. Also, to compound the bad news, Max would not now be able to attend the next block of sessions at 'Fun and Games at Golf,' as he called it, with his new best friend, Ben. He'd be devastated. She needed to call Sam and let her know. Ben would miss his sidekick, too.

CHAPTER SIXTEEN

THE SUMMER HEAT intensified, thickening the toxic soup pervading the London air. The windows to their twelfth floor office greenhouse opened only four inches wide—a safety measure to prevent them from jumping, Nathan reckoned. The weather stifled their work rate, but the firm refused to allow the air conditioning to be activated as it was too costly.

When Lucinda had declined Rebecca's request for two week's annual leave, Rebecca had bravely—foolishly, said Nathan—queried whether she could take a Monday off during the summer, eloquently reminding her employer that she had attended three Saturday training sessions and two Wednesday evening networking events. She would have welcomed the additional day to relieve the fatigue of the return journey from visiting her Dad.

However, she had been slapped down, back beneath her scummy stone, reminded that those events and seminars were obligations she'd been aware of when she had accepted the position, and all associates and partners were expected to contribute their own time, too.

"Has anyone ever requested to work part-time or job share at Baringer? One of the secretarial staff maybe?" enquired Rebecca of Georgina, the only approachable member of all the associates.

"Yes. The associate I'm replacing actually, Claris Freeman. She had a baby two years ago, struggled with the demands of working full-time coupled with the additional obligations of weekend training and late night social networking. So she requested part-time hours, three days a week to allow her to juggle the exorbitant cost of the private day nursery with her husband's job as a film cameraman, which frequently took him away from home. She is an extremely competent and well-respected commercial property lawyer with a large portfolio of satisfied corporate clients." Georgina tucked her short ebony curls behind her ears.

"Well, as you might guess, Lucinda didn't support her request and it was refused. So Baringer & Co has squandered her expertise and in doing so lost a number of high-profile commercial clients who followed her to her new practice at Fallows & Co, a more progressive law firm who agreed to a mixture of part-time and home-based working. They even developed a formal written, family-friendly, flexible working policy as part of their employees' terms and conditions. Not only for employees with young children, but also for those with elderly parents to care for. But then, Mark Fallows does have a disabled brother whom he helps care for, so he's bound to be more enlightened than these dinosaurs." She swung her arm in the general direction of Lucinda's office.

"Lucinda scaled the corporate mountain without assistance or flexibility whilst caring for her sister, so she's not going to countenance any slippage of the regime for us, is she? She's devoted her life to the firm, no dates, no self-indulgence of an annual holiday. Why should the company drag itself kicking and screaming into the twenty first century when there's a swarming herd of young, single lawyers prepared to overlook these discriminatory practices, clambering to move up the ladder to the exclusion of periphery concerns like family and children?"

"So if I were to ask for Tuesday afternoon off to attend Max's nursery's leaving presentation, she'd refuse?" Rebecca asked Georgina, but she already knew the answer.

"Don't even bother asking is my benevolent advice. It'd be better if she remained ignorant of the fact you were even considering attending—a black mark against Mrs Mathews' loyalty that you don't need. Try to stay in her good books, Rebecca. Keep your head down, work like crazy, endure the training, do the overtime, don't question the policies or politics, and don't mention you have any sort of life outside Baringer."

Georgina's chestnut eyes misted, but her strong features hardened. "Jonathan wants us to talk about having a family in the next year or so. I'm thirty-eight in November and the inevitable ticking is approaching crescendo. I agree with him, but I've just made associate. I want to go for partnership in a couple of years, which has been on my bucket list since school. It's blatantly obvious a lawyer can't fulfill both dreams here at Baringer."

A twang of sympathy reverberated in Rebecca's heart and she repeated her eternal missive of gratefulness for the presence of Max in her otherwise dull, dire life. She pulled free a smooth tendril of her tumbling amber locks from its tortoise-shell clip, slowly twisting it around her finger and thumb, running her finger down its silky, glossy tail.

"Georgina, I enquired about the company's policies for another reason, too. There's a friend I met at the Junior Golf Academy I take Max to, Sam Russell, who is CEO of Exquisite Forest, an ethical, environmentally-aware company which fashions handmade jewelry from sustainable, and if possible, organic sources—wood, bamboo, cotton, silk. In addition, they engage the services and purchase the products of 'kitchen table entrepreneurs', people who have caring responsibilities which keep them at home.

"Her company is seeking legal advice on the purchase of a warehouse in Manchester, initially for storage and distribution, but hopefully expanding to showcase their suppliers' products in small boutiques let on short tenancies. I can handle the property transaction but not the commercial advice. Do you think Lucinda would handle that? I only ask because of Exquisite Forest's ethical background."

"Anything to assist in making target and enlarging the client base would meet with Lucinda's approval, Rebecca," Georgina assured her. "And the introduction of such an important new client would earn you a few brownie points along the way. Well done!"

"Enough to give me Tuesday afternoon off? Max leaves nursery at the end of August, starts school in September. He really wants his mum there. Bradley's not interested, of course."

"It's your decision, but I wouldn't."

Georgina sloped off to wade through the towering pile of files on her desk, slaving her childless way toward striking one of her own items off her bucket list.

Rebecca didn't have the nerve to broach the subject of taking Tuesday afternoon off, so once again Max would be the undeserving victim of the firm's rigid policies and the choices she had made in her life thus far. She had no option. She needed this job. The salary was the only thing keeping a roof over their heads, so Max would sadly present his achievements to a room full of strangers.

[102]

"What did Georgina mean about Lucinda bringing up her sister? Didn't think she had any family. Thought she was 'married to the firm?'" Rebecca later queried when grabbing a tuna sandwich with Deb, the fount of all gossip.

"Not sure. There *is* a rumour she has a younger sister whom she helped raise, but I don't expect it to be true. She never mentions her, at least not to us minions. I did ask her once, years ago when I first started here, whether she had a partner or family and my head was slammed back below the parapet. Wouldn't dare ask again. You can though, if you like." She shot Rebecca a mischievous glance from under her long, dark, suspiciously false lashes.

"What do you think of this tiara?" Deb folded back the pages of the ubiquitous wedding glossy. "Is it too bling? I need to decide on my headpiece by next Wednesday, otherwise I won't have it for October. I still cherish the idea of something more unique, more natural, perhaps intertwined with fresh lilies. I just can't find the precise design I'm after. Something like this." Her hand glided across the thick, cream parchment as she sketched a circlet, intertwined with miniature lilies, primroses, and gyp.

"That's gorgeous, Deb. It's just you, hovering upon your long, flowing blonde locks like a halo! You'll be a flower-power bride. Will you float barefoot down the aisle or are we eventually gracing the Jimmy Choo wedding shoe emporium with our presence? I'm really excited. I'm going to try on *the* most sparklingly bling heels in the store!"

"It'll happen for you one day, Becky," said Deb, as she pinned the completed sketch onto her red division-board wall. "You'll stumble upon your own Prince Fergus if you stop searching and relax. I have every faith in you bumping into the right guy this time. But he could be lurking anywhere, so get out there and search, my girl! Any possibilities lurking in your interior design course?"

"All women, I'm afraid." Thank goodness. "I'm hooked though. Your stained glass panel is a work of art, even if I do boast my talents. I can't wait to solder the finishing touches. No details available until I unveil it on your wedding day."

"Give her a break, Deb. Always banging on about love, marriage, dating. 'Together Forever and Never to Split', it's all Hollywood baloney!" Nathan scowled.

"Hey, Mister Grouchy, if anyone lives in a fantasy world, that would be you, Nath. Where were you hanging out at the weekend? Tell Becky! No? Well, I will. At a Fantasy Fan Con. Attendees decked out as their chosen character from the books and the Hollywood film franchises of the fantasy world! Who did you dress up as, Nath?"

Nathan ducked his head and mumbled, "Snaaammmmm," as he flicked his biro between his fingers, pretending to concentrate on his computer screen.

"What? That famously grumpy wizard professor? Figures—not much makeup needed there then, Nath, eh?" As if sensing his discomfort, her voice mellowed. "Any more news on your mam?"

"Not long left, Mr McGovern, her consultant oncologist, says. Maybe six weeks, could be sooner. I'm shooting up to Edinburgh next weekend, but won't be taking Millie. I've heard no news from Emma's solicitors. It's too late now."

"What about issuing those court proceedings, Nathan?" Rebecca urged gently. "It may be too late for your mam to see Millie, but it's not too late for you and Millie to have a relationship. I could draft the documents tonight after work."

"It'll be a waste of time, but okay. Yes, please."

"We'll issue the application tomorrow. I'll come with you to the court appointment if I can clear it with Lucinda. It'll likely be the end of August when I get back from my week in Northumberland."

[104]

"Thanks, Becky." And he turned away sharply.

CHAPTER SEVENTEEN

THE END OF July marked the last of the adult and child taster sessions at Try Golf. Max badgered Rebecca to allow him to continue on to the Junior Golf Academy with Ben. She'd had to explain carefully to him that there wasn't any spare money—it was a lot more expensive than the taster sessions, which had been subsidised by the PGA to get more people into the now-Olympic sport, especially children and women.

She reminded Max they had a week's holiday in Northumberland coming up in a couple of weeks. She promised she'd treat him to a round of golf at the nine-hole course they were lucky enough to have in their village at Matfen. It was just along a country lane from Rosemary Cottage, where Rebecca had decided they would set up camp for the week as she couldn't afford a room at a B&B and wouldn't accept any more of Claudia's hospitality.

She'd need a machete to tackle the jungle of a garden, at least to improve the cottage's kerb appeal in the hope that passing summer holidaymakers and Hadrian's Wall ramblers fell under its spell just as she had.

"There's also a Go Ape in the woodlands near the cottage, Max. You can swing from the trees like a monkey on a zip-wire. Do you want to give that a go? We'll do lots of fun stuff together. Visit Granddad, hang out with Aunt Claudia, Rowan, Harry, and Daisy, take a trip to the cinema. Maybe go swimming?"

"Yes, yes, yes. But I still want to be Ben's friend, Mum."

"I know, Max, but you'll be starting reception class at St John's in September. You'll be busy making new friends there, too."

"But, Mum, Ben is so cool. I hate nursery. Stanley is still mean to me. He calls me horrid names because he says I haven't got a dad!"

Rebecca was stunned. "You have got a dad, Max sweetheart. He loves you very much."

"That's what I told Stanley, but he says that he never comes to collect me from nursery, or takes me on trips at the weekend like Daniel's dad does. That's why Stanley says I'm a bastard. I'm glad I'm not going to nursery anymore."

The anvil-sized thud to her chest caused Rebecca to bow forward, shocked beyond belief. *Because of my non-existent love life, Max has had to endure such callous and—frankly for such a young child— abhorrent name-calling.*

No four-year-old should have to be subjected to that. She resolved not to let the incident pass and vowed to raise the issue with Barbara Babcock on Monday when she dropped Max off. She swallowed her anger at the cruelty of children, but the balloon-sized lump of pain lodged in her chest.

"Well, let's enjoy this last session of golf, and afterwards we'll treat ourselves to a hot chocolate and a slice of chocolate cake in the clubhouse to celebrate, eh?"

[107]

"Yes, yes, yes."

"And what about a trip to the seaside tomorrow?" she offered on a whim, galvanised by Max's dreadful experience at the hands of Stanley. "Shall we invite Ben and his mum to tag along, too?"

"Yes, yes, yes." And he sprang off like a marionette, his miniature golf club in hand, to find Ben.

"Hi, Becky. How's things?" asked Sam. "Have you decided whether to enroll Max in the Junior Academy yet? Ben's keen and it'd be great if they could do the Academy together."

"I don't think so, Sam. He'll be starting school in September. I'm going to see how that goes. Maybe later on."

Sam was astute and accepting. She knew Rebecca struggled with finances. "Did you clear things with your boss to undertake Exquisite Forest's legal work? I'm anxious to get the ball rolling on the warehouse in Manchester, need it up and running for the Christmas season. I'd prefer you to handle the majority of the work, if you can."

"Lucinda is very keen to win your work. I'll start things off on Monday and, if you are available, I have set up an appointment for you for the day I get back from my week's holiday in Northumberland, August thirty first at three p.m."

"That's great. Thank you, Becky. You did ensure that Lucinda is aware of our company's ethics on environmental and working practices? It is important to us that we maintain our ethos in all our dealings with suppliers and partners."

"Lucinda Fleming is an excellent lawyer, an expert in her field and well-respected. I'm confident your legal work will be efficiently and sympathetically managed in accordance with your company's criteria. Thank you, Sam. It's good of you to trust your business to Baringer & Co."

She needed to have a conversation about Exquisite Forest's ethical standards and policies with Lucinda before Sam attended her appointment, but it wouldn't be the easiest subject to broach.

"Well, we weren't seeing eye-to-eye with our previous solicitors. Found some of their working practices, especially toward women, contradicted our philosophy. But as I see Baringer & Co has a female partner in Ms Fleming, they must be more progressive than our last law firm." She grimaced, flicking her short, graduated golden bob out of her eyes. "Fancy a coffee after the session?"

"I've already promised Max a hot chocolate and a slab of chocolate cake." She laughed. "As well as a trip to the seaside tomorrow. Mother's guilt—never bubbling too far from the surface. He's just confessed to being bullied by a boy at his nursery. I need to deal with that on Monday. I can't wait for him to start school. Only three weeks left at Tumble Teds for him. Then a week in Northumberland, camping out at the cottage, pottering in the weed-infested garden, and visiting my dad in his care home."

"Lucky you. I adore Northumberland—went there for our holidays as a child with my two brothers. We stayed in a caravan park, the one overlooking Bamburgh Castle, five of us in a four-berth caravan. Best holidays I've ever had, fishing in rock pools, storing starfish and tiny translucent crabs in bright yellow buckets with turrets, constructing huge sandcastles in the driving wind behind our red and white striped windbreak, burying Edward up to the neck in sand and leaving him there. Loved it!

"We spent the evenings playing board games or sat outside the village pub devouring beef crisps and drinking lemonade. I must persuade Ben and Angus to take a trip up there, rent a caravan, relive the nostalgia. Ben's travelled to all sorts of exotic places, Disneyworld, Majorca last year, but he's never experienced a good old British seaside holiday. Hey, could Ben and I come along with

[109]

you tomorrow to the seaside? Angus is away on business in Thailand at the moment and Ben would love it!"

"Max'd love it, too. We're learning how to skim stones—a special request of Max. Are you up to the challenge?" She thought of *The Little Green Book of Wishes* and smiled. Their new weekend bedtime ritual was studying the tips and pointers for the next day's chosen activity, or discovering that they could make up new challenges themselves, having been inspired by the book to think laterally. She'd never enjoyed reading with Max so much, no disrespect to Thomas and Percy.

ON A BLUSTERY but warm August Sunday, Rebecca, Max, Sam, and Ben found themselves chasing each other and the waves on the sandy beach at Southend-on-Sea. They constructed the most artistically 'grand-designed' sandcastle, not only with the obligatory moat and drawbridge, but with its own personalised mini-golf course, complete with paper British flags marking the holes. Sam rushed back to her ice-white, four-by-four, producing a putter and four balls and they enjoyed an hour of hilarity. Afterward, they launched onto the red tartan picnic rug scoffing their hastily-assembled, sand-infested picnic, hypnotised by the rhythmic crashing of the waves—nothing tasted better.

Max watched, fascinated, as two skinny teenage boys ambled by, headphones clamped to their ears, scanning the beach with metal detectors, occasionally stooping to investigate a heightened squeal emitted from the machines.

"Can I have a metal detector for Christmas, Mum?"

"We'll see, Max." She lovingly messed his hair, sand even ingrained on his scalp.

"You know, we've got one in our garage at home. Ben got it for his birthday last March. Rushed out to use the gadget a couple of times and never used it since! Why don't we lend it to you, Max, try it out, see if you like it, then you can decide if you want to include one on your Christmas wish list?"

Turning to Rebecca, who was valiantly brushing back her tousled hair as it whipped across her face while she finished the last triangle of her ice-cream cornet, Sam whispered, "He'll get bored with it, just like Ben has. I'll drop it 'round next week, have to sneak it in the car because as soon as Ben sees it again his interest will be piqued, and I'm never again spending the day trailing in the wake of a wailing metal detector!"

"Yes, yes, yes." Max bounced straight away before his mum could refuse the kind offer.

"Right, that's settled. Keep me updated with your treasure quest, Max! Come on, let's get some of those fabulous fish and chips. I'm still starving. The fresh sea air and the delicious aromas have wormed their way past my willpower. All this castle constructing and crazy golf tournaments is too much for an overworked CEO and aging mother."

CHAPTER EIGHTEEN

REBECCA DAYDREAMED WHILE looking through the kitchen window, the blurred and faded monochrome images of London's cityscape replaced with the countryside's vivid Technicolor idyll. Black-and-white Friesian cows grazed rhythmically in the lush green meadows, smiling buttercups swayed gently in the soft August breeze, watched over by a clear electric-blue sky.

For the first time in years a blanket of calm descended on her soul, her shoulders dropped two inches lower than her usual uptight stance. She finished rinsing the breakfast dishes, rubbed her soil-ingrained hands on the fluffy tea towel, and sauntered outside to survey the slow progress in the front garden.

The beige gravel path, scalped of encroaching weeds, had lifted the face of the cottage, but its lawns either side, flanked by the sweet-smelling rosemary bushes after which it was christened, were so whiskery she doubted the ancient, rusty lawnmower would win the battle to barber them.

Max was in his element racing around the garden with his new toy, the coveted metal detector, squealing whenever he heard the high-pitched beep. His little face had caught the sun from spending so much time outside in the garden and his skin appeared rosy and healthy, not peaky and pale. Not once had she witnessed his sleeve-chewing affliction, and because he was content, so was Rebecca.

The cottage demanded a colossal amount of work to make it habitable for any length of time, but the summer days were warm and long. Rebecca had declared it the camping holiday she had always promised Max they'd have. They were unable to use the back bedroom and she did pray it wouldn't rain whilst they were there, but they could always decamp to the lounge and sleep there.

Galvanising herself into action, she'd telephoned Jeremy Goldacre at the estate agency that morning to urge him to push the cottage hard during these essential summer weeks. This was the time when walkers and holiday makers descended on the region to walk Hadrian's Wall, soak up the history, or cycle the Coast-to-Coast—dipping the wheels of their cycles in the North Sea at one end and the Irish Sea at the other.

Surprised he deigned to speak to her himself, she'd endured the usual sales guff. But she experienced a spurt of assertiveness, reminding him the cottage had been on the market for over a year now, that when he had sold the property to her he'd promised buyers were queuing to snap up a piece of rural charm on the edge of the famous Roman Wall.

"Work harder," she snapped, "or I'll instruct another agent." When she replaced the receiver, the inevitable growl of guilt rumbled through her chest. It wasn't Jeremy Goldacre's fault she was in the position of being desperate for a sale. That had her own expertise written all over it.

Max and Rebecca resumed their mammoth gardening task. They concentrated their best efforts on the front garden and the all-important 'first impressions'. Digging together, each with an old wicker basket to collect the mounting weeds, each with an ancient trowel they'd found in the dilapidated shed at the bottom of the garden—an Aladdin's cave of rusting old garden implements, some of which Rebecca didn't recognize—abandoned by the previous owner.

Max had the stamina of a marathon runner, but Rebecca's neck ached, even her buttocks throbbed from the Pilates-like positions she assumed in reaching for recalcitrant weeds.

Rebecca had lost all sense of time as they dug for victory in the War of the Weeds, when a sharp insistent barking erupted from the little white garden gate and a black-and-white collie pushed it open with its nose, making a beeline for a terrified Max, frozen to the spot, eyes wide, trowel fallen from his hand.

"I'm so sorry," came an apologetic male voice. "Poppy, come back! Poppy!"

Poppy slunk reluctantly back to her owner, obediently parking her rear at her owner's feet, her soft brown eyes resting on Max.

"Are you staying here?" enquired the handsome stranger with disheveled flaxen hair. "I'm sorry about Poppy. She's a trainee sheepdog, so she's very trustworthy, never bites unless commanded!" assured her owner.

Max lurked behind Rebecca, eyeing Poppy suspiciously, chewing on the end of his t-shirt sleeve. Rebecca rose to her feet, brushing off the soil from her hands.

"Hi. I'm Rebecca Mathews and this is my son, Max." She draped her arm around Max's shaking shoulders. "Yes, we're staying here. Well, we're camping, to be more precise." She gestured to the roof.

"I'm Joshua Charlton, and, as you'll have gathered, this is Poppy." He offered his large, calloused hand to give Rebecca's soil-encrusted one a firm, confident squeeze, meeting her green eyes with his clear, blue smiling ones. His tousled hair stuck up at irregular angles, unintentionally trendy, a la surf dude! Tall, broad, rugby-player shoulders, he towered over Rebecca, but he carried his strong physique with the easy charm of someone comfortable in his own skin—all was well in his world.

"I'm sorry about Poppy, but she's used to a free run of this cottage and its once pristine gardens. The property belonged to High Matfen Farm until you bought it last summer. It's named after my mother, Rosemary Charlton." He bent down and grabbed Poppy's red collar to prevent her from dashing back into the garden, his worn green wax jacket, falling open to reveal a broad, muscular chest.

"Oh, I thought it was named that because of the profusion of rosemary plants!" Rebecca swung her palm toward the weed-choked garden.

"Mum loved this cottage. We rented it out in the summer to hikers and ramblers walking the Roman Wall, as well as golf enthusiasts—there're some fabulous courses around here, one on the doorstep at Matfen, but also two championship-standard courses, one at Slaley Hall and one at Close House.

"Mum passed away in February last year and the farm needed an injection of cash. Me and Dad didn't have the time or the creative ability to look after the cottage and its gardens, or to cope with the demands of the rental business, but still, it was a wrench when it was sold, particularly for Dad. It's good to see a family enjoying the place. Mum would have loved that. Not sure on her view as to the garden maintenance though." He threw her a mischievous smile, a twinkle in his cerulean eyes. "What happened to the roof?" His firm hand gestured to the sunken gable.

"It caved in during the February snow. I can't afford to get it fixed. Bit of cash injection needed into the Mathews household too." She laughed, glancing over at the For Sale board guiltily.

Josh didn't pry. "Is Max frightened of all animals or just dogs?"

"He's a non-discriminatory coward when it comes to animals, I'm afraid. He's not used to them, being a child of the grimy London suburbs. I'd love him to spend more time here, conquer his phobia, run free in the fields like I did when I was a kid."

"Well, why don't you visit the farm this afternoon? He can help me and Poppy corral the sheep—we've got thirty Northumberland Blackface sheep.

"These," he nodded toward the munching cows, "are Holstein Friesian cows, produce fabulous milk. Before Mum passed away, we kicked around the idea of producing our own ice cream commercially, using their milk and the organic fruit from our orchard at the farm and here at Rosemary Cottage. There's an orchard at the bottom of the back garden, you know, but, well, Mum became ill, and Dad and I have enough on our hands.

"Then there're the four mares we stable for the girls at Hexham riding school. That should give Max a varied introduction to the 'wild' animals of Northumberland!" He released a deep, throaty laugh.

Rebecca noticed his handsome, strongly-etched features, skin bronzed by the outdoor life in the summer sun, even in his ancient green wax jacket and mud-splashed wellies, she appreciated his bold, taut physique.

Josh did not fall into her preconceived image of a farmer's son, nor was he the usual type she found attractive, as far away from Bradley's immaculately groomed, self-image-obsessed smoothness as you could get. But that's what belied his charm. He had no self-conscious hang ups about his fashion choices, and what was the point undergoing a ridiculous monthly manicure, like Bradley did, when he was a farmer! In fact, she could almost envisage Josh and his rugby-playing pals swirling their pints of Irish ale, wrecking the questionable reputations of men like Bradley who only drank vintage champagne.

"He'd love to, and I would, too. Are you sure?"

"Dad'll enjoy having a young boy to show 'round the farm. See you later then, and bring the metal detector, Max. I'd love to have a go. There's been some interesting finds in this area being so close to the Roman Wall!"

CHAPTER NINETEEN

LATER THAT AFTERNOON, Rebecca and Max soaped off the mud from their horticultural toils and headed out for their daily visit to St Oswald's Lodge.

The familiar grip of guilt tightened her chest as she sped past the glorious façade of Morningside Towers, the lips of the pedestalled, winged horses guarding the entry gates snarling at her poor choice of care home for her father. She shoved her self-reproach to the recesses of her mind, recalling Claudia's assurances that George loved St Oswald. The food was homemade and wholesome, featuring his favourite steamed puddings, the staff were down-to-earth, motherly types, able to spare time for a chat about the old days or the residents' beloved families.

Still, Rebecca recollected the article Nathan had thrust under her nose in his copy of The Community Care magazine, which revealed devastating stories of the poor care and support provided by two residential homes catering for the needs of the elderly with dementia in the East Midlands. She'd studied the exposé with hot tears coursing down her cheeks, flabbergasted at the depths to which human beings could sink.

Rebecca had freaked out, powerless to upgrade her father's care to the desired Morningside Towers, the cheaper option of St Oswald's Lodge being necessary because of her own selfish decisions—her father, like Max, having to suffer the consequences.

It had taken Deb all her powers of persuasion, for which she was legendary, to calm Rebecca's frazzled nerves and reassure her there were no recorded issues with St Oswald. On the contrary, after forcing Rebecca to study their website, the home had received an outstanding report from its latest Care Quality Commission's inspection.

Nevertheless, she still held out for an imminent sale of Rosemary Cottage, and then a transfer for George to the luxurious Morningside Towers, where the staff wore crisp, white starched uniforms creating the impression of a swish health spa, rather than a residential care home for the elderly. But it would be months before she could achieve that aim, even if the cottage sold this summer. She had no other means of accomplishing her dearest wish—no self-respecting financial institution would part with its ill-gotten gains to a bankrupt and it was as unlikely as snow in August she would secure an increase in her salary. Even now, the fees for St Oswald's Lodge were mounting up. She dreaded the next overdue demand.

Max, familiar with the routine, shot off into the residents' lounge before her, in search of the only grandparent he had ever known. Her dad rested his spindly hand on Max's spiky head with love in his fading blue eyes. As he perched on the tapestry footstool next to his granddad, Max chattered away about his metal detector, his encounter with Poppy the sheep dog, and their invitation to visit the farm where they would embark on a quest for hidden treasure.

"Hi, Dad. How are you today?" She settled on his other side, drawing his cold, slender hand in her own.

"Oh, you know, Becky love, the old bones are creaking, but mustn't complain. It's better than the alternative." He smiled, slowly meeting her anxious green eyes. "Don't you worry about me, worry about this little one. He deserves to be in the hub of a happy, settled family, not rattling around with just the two of you in that lonely, dingy flat in London. He told me yesterday he hadn't seen his dad since Christmas. Is that true?"

"Bradley has a busy schedule, Dad," she started, but then relented. Why should she defend Bradley's disgraceful attitude toward his son? "You're right, Dad, you're right. It *is* my goal, you know. Deb and Nathan at work are cracking the dating whip, rest assured."

"Good, pet, good. How're those interior design classes going? Think you may have inherited that particular talent from me. Remember that potter's wheel I had when you were young? You loved moulding the sticky grey clay. And the kiln? Made your mum all sorts of modern ceramic art. Not sure she appreciated them all." He smiled weakly.

Rebecca had had this conversation with her dad every afternoon they visited St Oswald's Lodge that week, but she didn't care. She loved reminiscing with George, but she was concerned he was fading before her eyes. She wished with all her heart she was able to breathe some of her own life into his tired, skeletal body, restoring the dad she remembered as a child—strong, dependable, creative, but most of all fun!

"We're still designing our stained glass panels. Remember I told you I'm working on a piece for Deb and Fergus's wedding?"

But George had drifted off to sleep again, his chin slumped on his chest. Max jumped up from his perch.

"Granddad's sleeping now, Mum. Let's go to Josh's farm!"

Rebecca kissed her dad, placing his translucent hand on the red tartan blanket wrapped around his legs. She would have happily sat with him all afternoon, waiting for him to wake, resuming an identical conversation, but it wasn't fair to Max. She swallowed the threatening tears only as far as her chest where they merged with the lead weight already lodged solid there.

"Come on then, tiger. Let's pay those animals a visit."

"Yes, yes, yes," he said softly.

CHAPTER TWENTY

THEY SAUNTERED INTO the farmyard surrounded by a jumble of barns and outhouses, wellies squelching in the mud. Max had chattered excitedly in the car naming all the animals he would see, but as they approached the barn, he pulled back on Rebecca's arm, his sleeve end firmly in his jaw.

"I don't like those cows, Mum. They're huge. Can you carry me?"

Rebecca lifted Max onto her hip, his green frog wellies dangling around her legs, sketching lines of black mud across her ill-advised white jeans.

"Hi again! Hi, Max. Great to see you," called Josh from the farmhouse's paint-blistered front door, his smile relaxed and welcoming. "Let's start with the sheep. Poppy has done a great job rounding them up and they're waiting in the field behind the old barn."

On home turf, his presence exuded raw physicality. He had discarded the scruffy wax jacket—his broad muscular shoulders stretched his navy and crimson rugby shirt, open at the neck, revealing a suggestion of golden chest hair. His stride was long, measured, and confident as he led them, scampering in his wake, to the meadow behind the barn, delivering Rebecca the opportunity to study him from behind. Her eyes meandered to his firm, taut buttocks and she experienced a surprising jolt of sexual desire.

They had arrived at the field gate. Josh turned, catching Rebecca's eyes trained on his backside. She assumed her heated face matched her paprika-red roots.

Smirking, he reached out to collect Max from Rebecca's arms, balancing him on his own firm thigh, dangling him low to stroke the soft curly wool of the black-faced sheep. Initially tentative, Max's confidence blossomed as the sheep remained still, disinterested in the fondling.

"Can I take a sheep home for a pet, Mum?"

"It would certainly help keep the garden tidy. Not sure about the flowers though." Rebecca laughed, enjoying herself immensely, caressing the silky wool on the back of the sheep nearest to her. "Their fleeces are so velvety—do they produce wool as soft? I'd adore a hand-knitted jumper in this yarn!"

"Dad and I agreed that the only way the farm is going to survive into the future is to diversify. Unfortunately, we're not skilled in the craft of knitting." He laughed.

Rebecca tried to envisage Josh with a pair of wooden needles but the image was incongruous, his large hands seemed more adept at handling a rugby ball or grasping a struggling sheep between his firm legs than wiggling knitting pins. Again, she experienced an exquisite stab of lust as she easily visualised his long, muscular legs, naked, splattered in mud from a rugby field.

Pull yourself together, Rebecca.

"The reason we sold Rosemary Cottage after Mum passed away was to allow Dad and I to start the complicated process of drawing up plans and apply for planning permission for six properties—two barn conversions and four new, stone-built houses over in the bottom field, just beyond that oak tree."

Josh settled Max more securely on his hip, fastened the wooden gate, tying the posts with thick rope, and then they made their way back to the courtyard for lemonade.

"I studied structural engineering at university, loved it. Never a dull moment! The course encompassed a diverse spectrum of talents—maths, science, art, design, technology, geography, computing, take your pick. I worked for a cutting-edge company of structural engineers in London, a generalist at first as I learned the ropes, but my true interest lies in forensic engineering."

They perched at the ancient wooden patio table sipping cold lemonade, Max digging hungrily into a bag of salt and vinegar crisps, Poppy drooling by his side, chasing any stray morsel and producing fits of giggles from Max.

"I know what you mean about having a passion. Mine is for interior design. But what's forensic engineering?" Rebecca watched as Josh's bright blue eyes widened with enthusiasm, clearly relishing the opportunity to relive his passion. She selected a thick curl, twisting it slowly around her finger as she gave Josh her full attention.

"Often structures fail to perform. Some are damaged by natural disasters, such as floods or earthquakes, whilst others are destroyed by terrorism—the Twin Towers, for example. Some fail due to human error in the design or the build. By studying the process of collapse, we can learn how to build stronger, more resistant structures in the future."

"Why did you give that up? You speak so passionately about it."

His face softened, his eyes dropped to the cracked, silver-grey table, "Mum became ill—breast cancer—and Dad was struggling with the farm. It was a no-brainer really. Mum and Dad needed me here, so I came. That's why Dad agreed to sell Rosemary Cottage after Mum died and to pursue the application for planning permission for the properties—to create a project I could get my teeth into."

Josh spoke without a trace of bitterness or self-pity for the loss of what could have been a glittering career. "Alicia, my girlfriend at the time, refused to move 'up north', so we parted company. That was two years ago. She's married now, would you believe, expecting twins at Christmas.

"Anyway, we heard last week that planning permission has been granted, subject to numerous conditions. We're toying with selling a couple of the plots to self-builders, then to build the other two and complete the barn conversions ourselves, well, me mainly, as hands-on project manager. Dad thinks I need more hassle than the farm can throw at me!

"I spoke to the estate agent who handled Rosemary Cottage. He reckons he can sell the two self-build plots straight away, which would give us the start-up capital for the others.

"I have to say, I was surprised you snapped up the cottage without a full structural survey. I made it clear to Jeremy Goldacre there was an issue with the gable end, made sure he agreed to disclose this to any potential purchaser, even put this stipulation in writing. I see what I had anticipated happened with the first heavy snowfall."

Rebecca removed the end of her lock of hair from her mouth. "What? You told Jeremy Goldacre about the roof? He didn't mention anything to me about a problem with the roof when I viewed. He even said, in his expert opinion, it was a sound little investment, no need for an expensive survey. I paid cash so didn't need a survey for a mortgage. I realised buying without a survey was naïve, I should have known better, but at the time I made a number of stupid decisions and I just wanted the transaction to go through as quickly as possible." Her green eyes flashed.

Josh experienced a stirring in his stomach.

"Mind you, even if he had described the place as infested with rats and teeming with cockroaches, I would still have bought it. I had my head in the clouds and my brain in the deep freeze, dreaming of raising a happy family under its roof in the idyllic Northumberland countryside. Rosemary Cottage is so pretty, it sucked me in with its magic."

"Mum loved it, too. She tended that garden and its orchard until the day she died. It was her second child, Dad always teased her."

"I'm sorry about your mum. I lost my mum five years ago. Not a day goes by without a thought, a wish sent in her direction. My dad, George, lives at St Oswald's Lodge—we've just visited him, left him snoozing in the sunshine. He's frail but we reminisce every visit about his beloved Marianne."

"Yes, Dad struggles sometimes. He's a tough, rough-and-ready farmer. People don't expect him to have a gentle heart. But he's not prone to self-pity, so we both just get on with it. Bit worried about the current owner of Rosemary Cottage though and the deplorable state of its garden," he added mischievously.

"Dad's relinquishing the reins of the farm over to me step by step, keen to start on plans for diversification. I think the project has given him a new lease on life. I was surprised when he agreed we should apply for planning permission for the properties in the lower field, but he wants me to have a future at the farm. The other alternative was to sell up, for me to return to London, but I can't envisage Dad existing for long in a suburban semi in Newcastle. His world is here, amongst the animals he loves, and I have to admit so is mine, but the farming alone doesn't come close to breaking even."

He drained his glass, setting it on the table thoughtfully. "I'm concerned to hear Jeremy failed to disclose the issue of the gable end to you, especially after I specifically asked him to do so. He gave me his promise. Might speak to him about it. Dad knows Geoffrey Goldacre, his father—it's his estate agency business. Had it for the last forty years with his own father. Geoffrey Goldacre was always honourable in his dealings.

"Come on, Max. Let's try and get that metal detector buzzing. Lots of nooks and crannies to scout out in the farmyard and the fields. We might even find some treasure!" He dusted his hand over the top of his auburn head, just as excited as Max.

They rushed off ahead of Rebecca to collect the contraption from the back of her silver car, Josh's strong frame and long stride a contrast to Max's little legs as they peddled to keep abreast of him. Knowing men and boys loved any new gadget, she decided to resume her bum-numbing seat in the courtyard and await their return.

She turned her face toward the warm sunshine, basking in the peace and tranquility, broken only by the grumble of a cow ready to milk and an occasional high-pitched squeal from the metal detector or Max, she wasn't sure which.

Twenty minutes later, they returned to the courtyard laughing and shouting. Max darted up to her, his hand full of 'treasure'—an assortment of rusty nails, screws, and the fantastic find of an old pitted silver horseshoe.

"Look, Mum, a horse's shoe. Josh says I can keep it. It's real treasure, you know. Josh says the shoe will bring us luck!" He rushed over to the stone drinking trough to scrub the silver arc to a shine. Josh perched on the bench, so close to Rebecca her hair follicles rose.

"Max informs me he wants to go to the village school here in Matfen because a boy called Stanley bullies him at nursery. Is that true? I thought bullying was stamped out in schools these days as soon as it rears its ugly head?"

"I know about Stanley. I've spoken to Max's keyworker." She pulled a face at the ridiculous label. "They've assured me they will supervise the 'situation' more closely. But he's finished at the nursery now except for a few days next week, after which he starts reception class a week on Tuesday.

"I agree, though. Max would love to start school here. The village school must be a heavenly place to learn. But Max's dad, my ex, lives in London and I don't want to prevent them from having a relationship by relocating here."

Max's beaming face appeared at the worn old bench where they were chatting. "Remember you promised to take me to that Hadrian's Wall, Josh! Next time we come? Will we see Scottish people climbing over it to get into England to steal our treasure?"

"You never know, Max," said Josh with a smile.

CHAPTER TWENTY-ONE

"HI, CLAUDIA! THANKS for inviting us to dinner." Rebecca hugged her steadfast friend before grabbing a seat at the family's kitchen table, strewn with the detritus of childhood activities. "I couldn't be hassled to cook tonight. Max and I visited Dad at St Oswald this afternoon. He's so frail now. He usually manages to stay alert for our afternoon visits, but he fell asleep after just half an hour today — after berating me about still sticking it out in London with Max and my failure to find a decent guy to settle down with," she added wryly.

"I'm concerned about him, Claudia. When we return to London on Saturday, I won't be able to get back up to Northumberland for a couple of weeks—need to get Max settled in at school. And I promised Lucinda I'd attend a networking event after my week's leave, too. Deb wants to finalise her wedding shoe choices, narrowed down to three spectacular, but extortionately priced specimens. Nathan's court hearing is next Tuesday and I promised to represent him. What if anything happens and I can't get up here in time?"

"Daisy and I will continue to visit him every day, Becky," Claudia promised. "Despite your obsession with the sumptuous 'Morningside Spa', he's being well cared for at St Oswald. Volunteers visit to read newspapers and books to them, and to offer a little help to those who need it to eat their meals. When I get this little one"—she jiggled Daisy on her lap—"off to school, I'm going to volunteer there." She flicked back her shiny black hair and smiled at Rebecca's permanently anxious face.

The Scott household had decamped to the patio to enjoy the last rays of that day's sunshine. The Wedgewood-blue wooden table was laid with white china plates awaiting the arrival of Paul to carve the roast leg of lamb, bedecked with copious branches of rosemary from Rebecca's cottage garden. The delicious aroma wafted from the Aga to the back garden, making tummies rumble.

"Harry's desperate to see Max. Our rabbit was lonely and has a mate now—Mopsy and Graeme. Don't ask! I think it's the PE teacher at his school, but he insisted. What's in a name! I'm surprised at Max cradling Graeme though. Thought he had an all-things-soft-and-fluffy phobia?"

"Guess where we've been this afternoon?" Rebecca posed coyly. "To pet the farm animals at High Matfen Farm, next to the cottage. The farmer's son stopped by earlier this morning—out strolling with his collie, he said. He invited Max to join in with rounding up the sheep. He wasn't sure at first, but he soon got stuck in with Josh encouraging him. Did you know Rosemary Cottage was not named in honour of the herbs lining the garden path at all? It's named after Josh's mother, who tended and cherished the garden up until she passed away. The place cast its spell on her, too."

[130]

As Rebecca had anticipated, Claudia latched on immediately at the mention of a farmer's son. "What's he like? All rugged handsome features, outdoorsy with powerful flexed muscles from the hard, physical labour tending the fertile fields, but gentle and resourceful when tending more intimate fertile areas?" She swooned theatrically, taking a swig from her deep velvety Merlot.

"Very funny, Claudia. But he's okay, you know. Max achieved huge strides in conquering his fear. I'm so proud of him. Josh has promised him a ride on one of the horses next time. I'm not so sure about that though. They're colossal—a head taller than me, but Josh could look them in the eye. Max is up for it, would you believe?"

They wandered into the warmth of the kitchen to top up their glasses, settling into the more comfortable folds of the sofa, the news miming on the TV in the background whilst the children chased the rabbits around the garden, the occasional scream signaling all was well.

The TV screen flashed live to a man balancing precariously on the top reaches of London's Tower Bridge clad in a wizard costume, complete with striped scarf and black pointed hat.

"Turn the sound up, Claudie, please."

The camera zoomed in to highlight a hand-drawn banner brandished by the protester—"F4J—SUPPORT A CHILD'S RIGHT TO SEE ITS FATHER!"

"You know, I have a certain amount of sympathy for those guys. Remember Nathan in our office? He's desperate to see his daughter, Millie. Hasn't seen her since Christmas and that was only so his ex could collect Millie's presents from him. Whenever Emma has a man in her life, she severs all contact with Nathan. But the worst thing is his mother is very ill. She lives in Edinburgh and would dearly love to see her only grandchild before she moves on to the festival in the sky. Nathan has coaxed, cajoled, pleaded, and begged Emma, but she either refuses or ignores him all together.

"She's currently enjoying the advances of a rugby-playing boyfriend who terrifies Nathan out of his wits, but he's bravely agreed to start things moving on a legal basis. The first court appointment is listed for Tuesday next week. Lucinda has agreed to allow me to accompany him, to represent him at the hearing, as long as I work back the time I lose whilst out of the office.

"But look at that guy, how desperate must he be to have contact with his children to don a costume and scale the Tower Bridge in the sure and certain knowledge he'll get arrested and that in itself will be fuel for his ex to refuse contact." Rebecca shook her head.

"Then look at Bradley, not the slightest interest in forming a relationship with his son, never mind maintaining one! Nathan hates him with every bone in his body and he's never laid eyes on him!" she added with a mirthless laugh.

The phone buzzed in the hall.

"Oh, that'll be Paul. He must have been held up at work, he's usually home by now. It seems you'll be responsible for the carving tonight, Becky." Claudia swished the air with an imaginary knife. "Can you look out on the kids? Round them up, hands scrubbed, for dinner."

Claudia was only absent a couple of minutes before returning to the kitchen, her pale face blanched further and shock etched across her dark features.

"That was Jean Peters from St Oswald's Lodge, Becky. Your mobile must be off. Your dad's had another stroke. He's on his way to the hospital now." She laid her hand on Rebecca's shoulder, tears rolling down her cheeks. "Leave Max with us. You get off to the hospital. Are you okay to drive?"

"Oh, erm, yes. Thanks, Claudia. I'll ring." And she shot off, kissing the top of Max's head as she ran through the scarlet front door—sending up a prayer to the still clear, cerulean skies.

CHAPTER TWENTY-TWO

THE HOSPITAL WAS eerily silent at that time of night with none of the hustle and bustle of visiting time, which had ended an hour ago. Disoriented, Rebecca blinked, forcing her red-veined, tear-swollen eyes to become accustomed to the neon glare of the deserted corridors.

She was the only person Dad had to support him in these worst of circumstances—alone in a strange, unfriendly, and frightening place. She needed to establish which ward he had been taken to, to be there for him, clasp his hand in hers, force her strength and vitality into his failing body, and comfort him as he had her over the years, throughout her appalling choices and awful decisions.

One of the nursing staff directed her to a side ward where her father lay motionless, sleeping quietly against three puffed up pillows—a frail figure, a shadow of his former sturdy presence— hands folded neatly upon the starched cotton sheet, looking withered, sprinkled with age spots.

Was the fact he'd been allocated his own side room an ominous sign? Her heart fluttered in her chest, a lump of panic forming like a recalcitrant pebble in her throat. She slumped into the brown leather visitor's armchair adjacent to his bedside, drew his cool, smooth hand into hers, careful not to dislodge the IV line, and waited.

She must have drifted to sleep, her head on her dad's hand. It was six a.m. when she woke. The nursing staff was changing shift— just another day at the coalface of clinical care. She combed her fingers through her knotted hair, securing errant wisps behind her ears. Her father remained motionless, sleeping on peacefully, his life dependent on a multitude of wires and tubes.

Deciding to search for coffee to inject life into her sluggish brain and freshen up before locating the doctor or nurse in charge, she unfurled her aching muscles. As she hadn't been able to take everything in last night, only managing to nod blankly at Dr Patel, unable to register the simplest of explanations, she would seek reassurance from the new staff on duty. She had caught herself wishing Bradley was at her side, if only for the warmth and support of another human being.

She remembered the doctor's warning that her father had had a major stroke, and that as he hadn't yet regained unconsciousness, the next forty-eight hours would be crucial. They were unable to give an accurate prognosis, but he was being carefully monitored.

She resumed her lonely vigil at his bedside, gazing out the hospital window to the housing estate beyond. Lights popped on as the world resumed its daily routine, oblivious to the radiating sorrow from the hospital in their midst.

If wishes were reality, George would rouse and pat her clammy hand—her dad from childhood—sturdy, down-to-earth, sensible, and the only person she could rely on to tell her the truth, to cut straight to the chase. This he had dispensed in her direction many times, but she had blithely ignored those pearls of wisdom she professed to cherish. He had counseled her to relocate back to Northumberland when she and Bradley separated, where they could have plugged the gap in each other's lives, supporting each other, supporting Max.

But she'd chosen Bradley's non-existent relationship with Max over a loving relationship with his only grandfather. Once again, her choices had proved erroneous.

George had endorsed her decision to purchase Rosemary Cottage, but had gently warned her that it was not guaranteed to produce her desired outcome. A mere building could not deliver a happy, loving family, no matter how beautiful the ivory roses draped around the door were. He had been right again.

Her cluttered thoughts swirled around her befuddled, sleep-deprived brain as she slowly twisted her disheveled locks through her fingers, pulling harder, winding tighter. Without her dad in her life, she and Max had to face the world alone. The thought terrified Rebecca. Did she have the courage to take on the world for them both? She resumed her anxious prayers because she just wasn't ready to be an orphan.

The hospital existed in a time warp. She lost all track of time until mid-morning when she perceived a slight shake of her dad's hand and heard a faint groan. She hurriedly gestured the duty nurse to his bedside.

"How are you, Mr Phillips?" the stout nurse asked gently, checking his monitors.

A faint squeeze of her hand signaled Rebecca to lean toward him. "Hi, Dad. It's me. How are you feeling? You're in the hospital, but you're doing fine." A blatant lie. His pale, watery eyes opened and his head rotated on the mountainous pillows to gaze at

Rebecca, his beloved only child. Holding her anxious, green eyes with his own, he smiled. She had her mother's eyes, she knew. His eyes closed slowly and once again he was motionless, tranquil.

Rebecca maintained a constant stream of inconsequential chatter, hoping George could hear her, that he would open his eyes and smile at her again, but he made no further movement. At nine p.m., after Saturday's visiting hours ended, the same sturdy nurse, still on her shift, ordered Rebecca home to get some rest. She promised a call if there were any developments.

Reluctantly, Rebecca agreed. She had to explain to Max about Granddad and reassure him she was okay. A busy schedule had been organised by Claudia and Paul to distract him from the inevitable anxiety for his absent mum and ailing Granddad at the hospital, but he would be fretting for her return.

"HI, MAX SWEETHEART. Had fun with Harry and the rabbits today?" Rebecca stroked his tufted hair, overwhelmed with love for her child as he clutched the much-loved Harrods bear, apparently now named George.

"Yes, Mum, but I worried all day about Granddad. Why is he at the hospital?"

"He's very poorly, Max. His heart is weak, but the doctors and nurses are looking after him really well. He's in safe hands. Come and tell me about your day whilst we share a huge bubble bath." She raised her eyes to Claudia's.

"I'll get the bubbles started whilst Mum grabs a bowl of that hot minestrone soup." She smiled, touching Rebecca's shoulder.

As she settled a cheerier Max into his Thomas & Friends inflatable bed, exhaustion and trauma, highlighted by the soft caress of the fragrant bath bubbles, threatened to overwhelm her.

Rebecca returned to the kitchen where she slumped in the chair next to Claudia, hugging the remnants of a strong black filtered coffee, and trawled through the harrowing events of the last twenty-four hours.

"Lucinda would only authorise one week's leave during the summer break. I requested two so I could settle Max in at school, but was refused. I'm due back on Monday."

"She can hardly refuse you compassionate leave! Your father's had a stroke, for goodness sake, lying unconscious in hospital. She's the cat's devil if she demands you return to work on Monday."

"I don't have any choice. I can't risk losing my job, Claudie, and you know why. I'd never be employed by another legal firm. Who would take me on when there are trainee solicitors scrabbling around like rats at a feast, prepared to work for peanuts to scale the first rung of the ladder? I'm still amazed that Lucinda agreed to offer me a position, considering the circumstances. I've got an appointment set up with Sam Russell, the girl I met at the golf club. She's planning to instruct Baringer & Co to handle all her company's commercial business. It's a boost to our client base after we lost a host of clients when Claris Freeman decamped to Fallows & Co. I'm scheduled to meet her at three p.m. on Monday. I don't want to let her down. She's keen to get the business transactions moving."

"She'll understand, Becky. She was a friend first, before a business client."

"I don't know what to do. I have to stay in Northumberland, Claudie. Max has another week before he starts school. I'd never forgive myself if anything happened to Dad while I was in London and I couldn't get back here in time. Me and Max are all the family he has." The tightly sealed floodgates burst open and tears coursed down her translucent cheeks, her bony shoulders quivering with debilitating grief. She was grateful Max was tucked up in bed, spared of the trauma of witnessing his mother's defenses crumble.

"Oh, what if we lose him, Claudie? Before I've been able to set everything right? The cottage, the care home, our relocation back up to Northumberland, the happy settled family he wanted so much for me and Max. I've failed him totally."

Claudia hugged Rebecca to her chest, shards of her mahogany hair mingling with Rebecca's limp, dark auburn locks.

"Look, Becky, your dad loves you and Max. Every time Daisy and I visit, he tells us how proud he is of what you have achieved and that he adores Max. You're exhausted. Get some sleep. Here's the duvet." Claudia fussed around, tucking her in on their over-stuffed sofa. "It's Sunday tomorrow. Paul will entertain the kids and I'll come up to the hospital with you in the morning. Stop beating yourself up about the past—you can't change it. Before we leave you're going to contact Lucinda to request a week's compassionate leave."

"I don't relish that call, but yes, I will. I owe it to Dad to stay as long as I can."

She didn't expect sleep to arrive, preferring instead to rotate her numerous failures around in her mind, dissecting each one for maximum self-recrimination—a favoured pastime of hers. But as she'd only catnapped since Friday morning, she descended into the welcome oblivion sleep provided.

"WELL, I AM sorry to hear about your father, Rebecca. I hope he is receiving the appropriate care. However, I can only agree to two days compassionate leave. Company policy. I'll expect you at your desk on Wednesday morning. You say your father is unaware of your presence and unable to communicate. In my view, it is a pretty pointless activity sitting in vigil by his bedside all day."

Rebecca disagreed but held back the negative comments that sprang to her mind. She craved the opportunity to stay with her father in Northumberland for as long as possible, but she needed her job at Baringer & Co to pay her rent and keep a roof over her and Max's heads. She also had to consider Max's wellbeing, slot him back into his routine for school the following week. In addition, she had Sam's business issues to deal with. She was grateful for the trust Sam had placed in her professional abilities and determined not to fail her.

The grant of two days leave meant she'd miss Nathan's court appointment on Tuesday. She had promised him she would support him, but she'd be letting him down, too. And whilst Claudia didn't mind in the slightest, she had trespassed on her hospitality and child care provision for too long. She couldn't return to the cottage—it was too far away if she got an urgent call and had to rush to the hospital.

"Thanks, Lucinda. I will see you on Wednesday. Before I go, one of my friends, Sam Russell of Exquisite Forest Company, is due in at three p.m. tomorrow to discuss the purchase of a warehouse in Manchester. I mentioned the matter to you last week. I can reschedule her appointment for Wednesday, if you wish."

"No, don't. I'll deal with the transaction myself. His business needs can't be allowed to suffer because of your personal crisis. Goodbye." In her exhausted state, Rebecca failed to grasp the fact that Lucinda had assumed Sam to be Samuel and not Samantha until after the phone call ended.

In any event, the short conversation left her drained of all emotion except relief and gratitude that she was able to spend another two days at her father's bedside. She couldn't even summon up the energy to resent Lucinda's lack of empathy. Maybe she was right. There had been no indication that her father was aware of her presence since he had squeezed her hand on Saturday morning. She was unable to contribute anything to the improvement of his health. But if he could sense her presence at all, then she would be there.

Dabbing her eyes, Rebecca drew a steadying breath. The next call would be even more difficult.

"Hi, Nath. It's Becky here."

"Oh, hi, Becky. What are *you* doing ringing on a Sunday morning? What have you heard?"

"Erm, I've not heard anything. Look, Nathan, my father had a stroke Friday night. He's being treated in hospital here in Newcastle. He hasn't regained consciousness yet and I need to be at his bedside when he does. I've just endured a call to Lucinda and she's authorised two days compassionate leave. I'm due back at work on Wednesday."

"Only two days? Would it have been too much for the frozen dragon to give you a week off? I hope your dad's going to be okay, Becky."

"Nathan, the time off means I won't be able to attend the court appointment with you on Tuesday. I'm so sorry to let you down. Do you want to request a week's adjournment so I can come with you next week?"

"Don't worry, Becky, I totally understand. I can identify with what you are going through. I'll attend the hearing myself. I'm up for it now. Don't worry about me. Concentrate on what you have to do. For once in your life, stop worrying about everyone else. Take care of number one!"

"Thanks, Nath. Bye"

Tears coursed down her cheeks again, but her tumultuous emotions didn't prevent her from wondering what he had meant when he'd answered the phone demanding to know what she'd heard.

CHAPTER TWENTY-THREE

THE SUN BLEACHED the late August sky, its aquamarine canopy dotted with candy-cotton wisps of white clouds, spreading its increasing warmth through the twelfth floor windows of Baringer & Co. Pigeons cooed contentedly on the ledges until spotting a discarded morsel to retrieve.

"Where is Rebecca's three o'clock client?" Lucinda demanded.

"Over there, Ms Fleming." Baringer's pretty-but-dim receptionist indicated with a waft of her elegantly manicured hand to where Sam was perched on the corporate black leather couch, her slender legs crossed at her ankles.

"No, Louise. I'm waiting for Mr *Sam* Russell, CEO of Exquisite Forest Company." Lucinda rolled her eyes, chastising Louise in her most condescending voice.

"Oh, no, it's *Mrs* Sam Russell, Ms Fleming." Louise helpfully emphasised the Mrs, flashing her perfect white teeth at Sam who had stood up, realising Lucinda Fleming's confusion. She offered her hand.

"Samantha Russell, Exquisite Forest Company. I was expecting an appointment with Rebecca Mathews, though."

"Yes, well, Mrs Mathews is unfortunately unable to attend your appointment this afternoon. Personal crisis. But rest assured I have insisted she return to her desk on Wednesday. I will handle your instructions myself and bring Mrs Mathews up to speed when she returns."

"A personal crisis? What's happened?" Sam looked from Lucinda to Louise, anxious for news on her friend's predicament.

"Her father has had a stroke. He's hospitalised in Newcastle. Come this way, please, and we'll get down to business. I understand you are wishing to purchase a warehouse in Manchester?" Lucinda swept down the glass corridor toward her corner office, expecting Sam to follow in her perfumed wake.

"Hold on a moment, please. Rebecca's father is in hospital and you have granted her two days leave?"

Lucinda mistook Sam's alarmed expression for irritation that her business matters would be compromised.

"Yes, I know it's inconvenient, but I can assure you your company will not be delayed in your legal transactions due to her unexpected absence, Mrs Russell." Lucinda held open her office door for Sam.

"No, you misunderstand me, Ms Fleming. If Rebecca's father is in hospital, I'm surprised she's not attached to his bedside. She adores her father. She and Max are the only family he has!" Sam narrowed her indigo eyes at Lucinda. "First, you mistake me for a male CEO. Now I'm hearing that you refused a valued employee compassionate leave after her father is admitted to hospital following a stroke from which he has yet to regain consciousness.

Did Rebecca not explain to you Exquisite Forest's company ethos? EFC takes pride and is meticulous in ensuring our employees' wellbeing. We employ flexible working practices to allow for just this occasion. We find our employees work harder and the flexibility allows them to retain the work and life balance necessary for maximum productivity, as well as providing us with a contented, loyal workforce.

"My company cannot instruct a firm of solicitors which does not follow a similar workplace philosophy. Such archaic attitudes are exactly the reason we've chosen to remove our business from Harris and Strider."

"Rebecca did not discuss those issues with me, but I can assure you that your legal and business requirements will be delivered with care and skill, efficiently and expeditiously. That's the ethos you can expect from Baringer & Co. The bottom line is what it's all about, I'm sure you agree, Mrs Russell." She smiled.

"No, that's not what *our* business is all about, Ms Fleming. I'm sorry to disappoint Rebecca, but I am unable to engage the services of Baringer & Co to conduct our company's legal affairs, nor for the formation of the new company I had hoped to instruct you on today. Goodbye, Ms Fleming."

She turned, ignoring the stunned expression on Lucinda's face as she keyed in Rebecca's mobile number whilst waiting for the elevator.

Lucinda had the grace to blush as she overheard Sam Russell's voicemail message.

"Hi, Becky, Sam here. I'm so sorry to hear about your father and if there is anything I can do to help, please ask. Just met with one of Baringer & Co's partners who thinks she's kindness itself by granting you two days leave. Take care, Becky, do what you have to do. Speak soon."

During the lift ride to the lobby, Sam couldn't help but wonder why Rebecca didn't move on when she had such an antiquated boss.

CHAPTER TWENTY-FOUR

TUESDAY DAWNED AS an insult, its bright sunny rays painfully piercing Rebecca's desolation. She showered and dressed like an automaton, grabbed a coffee, and left for the hospital.

There had been no change whatsoever in George's condition. The doctor assured her they were doing all they could to make him comfortable, but there was no mention made of treatment or improvement.

This would be the last visit Rebecca would make until she returned to Northumberland after work on Friday night—too late for a visit. She and Max planned to leave at three p.m. at the latest for the exhausting return journey to Hammersmith. They'd have to wake at six on Wednesday morning—Max bundled off for his last three days of endurance at the dreaded Tumble Teds, and Rebecca loyally at her desk for nine.

That Tuesday morning, Max had begged to stay at Claudia's, desperate not to return to nursery and Claudia had pleaded with her to relent. Only three days remained of the summer holidays and her offer did provide a solution to Max's prayers.

After a further, lacklustre argument about not taking advantage of Claudia's hospitality, Rebecca had gratefully agreed. The journey was a nightmare for Max, strapped into the booster seat where he quickly became bored of the cornucopia of books and games Rebecca piled onto the back seat—the loop of nursery rhyme CDs grating the nerves after their fourth run through. It would also mean Max not having to return to Tumble Teds, allowing Rebecca to work late Wednesday through to Friday to repay the additional time off, zooming back up north as soon as she was released from her desk chains on Friday night.

Pausing at the door of her father's hospital room, her mind wandered back to happier times when her mum was alive and her father was the centre of her universe. As an only child, she'd enjoyed their undivided attention, thrived on it, her confidence and self-esteem as a young girl under their loving guidance more advanced than as a self-directed adult.

She sank into the familiar dung-coloured chair, wondering how many bottoms had rested on its shiny surface over the years, grasping her dad's limp, wrinkled hand with her cool, smooth one and allowing hot tears to flow unchecked. She murmured quietly to George, fanning the flames of childhood memories, of the adventures they'd had—the time she'd flown down a hill on her old blue bicycle, legs raised high, then crashing into the side of an old chestnut tree and receiving a broken arm for her daring. The resulting plaster cast had been the cause of proud boasting and autographs.

Time to leave arrived more quickly than she anticipated in the vacuum of hospital life. She bent her head to kiss George's forehead, her hair brushing his immobile face. She yearned for the excruciating pain, now settled anvil heavy in her chest, to fade.

"Goodbye, Dad. Off to the grimy streets of London. See you Saturday morning. Claudia promises to visit tomorrow. I love you."

SHE RACED TO Rosemary Cottage to secure the doors and windows and retrieve her holdall. When she had left the cottage four days earlier—a lifetime ago—for dinner at Claudia's, she'd expected to return that night.

Flinging her black leather satchel and the hastily stuffed overnight bag onto the back seat, she slammed the passenger door of her battered, old silver vehicle shut. As she sprinted to wrench open the driver's door, she stretched out her limbs, preparing for the interminable return journey to Hammersmith and the cold poky flat awaiting her arrival, an even more depressing thought minus Max.

Just as she slotted her jean-clad leg into the car, she spotted Josh with Poppy lolloping beside him, meandering along the lane, smiling. Despite everything going on in her crappy life, she returned his smile.

"Hi, Becky. In a rush? Where's Max?" he puzzled, his forehead creased in concern.

"He's staying over with my friend, Claudia, for a couple days. I'm…" She couldn't go on. To explain the last few days to Josh, who held her gaze so fondly, was too painful. She couldn't do it without breaking down.

He strode forward, draping his bulky arm clumsily around her shoulders, dwarfing her by his size. He dragged her slight frame into an embrace. "Is Max okay? What's wrong? What's happened?"

She leaned into him, feeling safe and protected from the cruel world beyond his arms, inhaling the tangy, citrusy aroma she recognised as one of her favourite colognes. Why couldn't she just stay here, wrapped in his scruffy, moss-green jacket, cocooned from life's torture forever?

There was an unidentifiable quality in this handsome man's genes that spoke directly to her soul and she no longer wanted to fight the urge to unload her misery. After all, he had known the sadness and grief of his mother's illness and passing.

The words tumbled out.

"It's Dad. He's had a stroke. He's in the Freeman Hospital, hasn't regained consciousness yet. Spent every day since Friday at his bedside, praying for him to improve. Nothing, though. I'm exhausted. Max is back to gnawing his sleeve. Now I'm travelling back to London because my boss only agreed to two days compassionate leave—due back at work tomorrow morning, nine a.m. sharp. I have to return because I'm desperate to keep my job. I can't afford to contradict Lucinda.

"Thank goodness for Claudia and Paul. They've agreed to look after Max until I can get back up here on Friday night—save him from the eight hours of motorway boredom." Her words of explanation came out in a whoosh of pain, tears rolling in well-worn tracks down her pale cheeks.

Even though Josh wouldn't have a clue who she was referring to, she gulped in a breath and continued, "And I've let my friends, Nathan and Sam, down. Missed a promised business appointment with Sam, a court hearing with Nathan. I'm a truly awful friend, a dreadful mother, and daughter. I'm a useless employee, too, whilst were on the 'Rebecca is a failure' subject, which quite frankly could go on forever."

[150]

"Come on, back inside. A cup of extra strong tea is prescribed by Doctor Josh Charlton. I can't allow you to travel to London in this fettle." He guided her along the weed-free path into Rosemary Cottage's kitchen, swiftly producing a huge brown teapot of strong Yorkshire tea—Rebecca's favourite—rinsing the discarded mugs in the Belfast sink whilst Poppy made a beeline for the stone-cold Aga, giving it a disgusted sniff.

"Used to be her favourite place when Mum was around. She'd come down to clean the cottage before the re-let to the next set of walking or cycling enthusiasts, and of course, the Aga was always lit to welcome them from their days spent rambling the length of the Wall. Poppy's not daft—it was the warmest place in the house." Josh scratched Poppy's floppy black ears affectionately. "Can I offer any help, Becky? Now or whilst you are away in London?"

"Thanks, Josh, you are kind. I don't suppose I can expect a mad rush of prospective buyers demanding to view the cottage. It's the last week of August, and anyway, the place is a complete mess. Come to think of it, Dad can't sign the documents even if a buyer is found, can he?" Rebecca lowered her gaze to her hands where she concentrated on scrapping skin from the sides of her thumbs in an effort to master her emotions.

"I thought the cottage was yours?" Josh asked, sipping from his mug of tea.

"It's a long story, perhaps for another day. But thanks again for your offer."

His eyes crinkled at the corners and he gave her wrist a tight squeeze. As he rinsed the mugs, his broad, muscular back strained the seams of his black and scarlet rugby shirt. His burly presence looked completely out of place as he washed up at a kitchen sink.

Josh wiped his hands dry on an old, linen tea towel. "Here's my mobile number and the farm's landline. Anything me or Dad can do to help—ring." After hesitating for a fraction of a second, he delved into his jeans pocket, producing a postcard decorated with sprigs of rosemary and thyme, the promised numbers scribbled in bold ink on the reverse, as he guided a calmer Rebecca to the waiting vehicle.

Rebecca studied the card, puzzled that he already had his contact details handy and that they were written on such a pretty card.

"Oh, yes, I was on my way to push this through your letterbox when I bumped into you. Found these postcards in an old, oak bureau at the farm—they must have been Mum's."

REBECCA WAS RUNNING late. If she didn't step on the gas she wouldn't arrive at her flat until well past midnight. She squeezed the accelerator for as much speed as the clapped-out, old rust bucket of a motor could generate.

Her stomach rumbled angrily as she approached the Motorway Service Station at Wetherby. Realising she should grab some snacks to keep her awake on the long, lonely journey—even missing the distraction of the interminable nursery rhymes—she aimed the car up the motorway exit road.

As she drew out a note for the cashier to pay for the mountain of unhealthy snacks she'd amassed from the store's aisles, her mobile buzzed to life. She toyed with ignoring the irritating noise—she needed to put some miles on the clock and she did not recognise the caller's number—but she jabbed the answer button anyway as she walked to the car.

"Hi."

"It's Doctor Patel from the Freeman Hospital. Is this Mrs Rebecca Mathews?" His Indian accent sounded more pronounced over the phone.

"Yes." Her breath wrenched from her constricted throat.

"I'm afraid I have to impart the sad news that your father has passed away. I'm very sorry for your loss, Mrs Mathews. He hadn't regained consciousness, he just slipped away peacefully. I'm on duty until ten p.m. this evening. Please, advise the staff nurse when you arrive and I'll meet with you. My heartfelt sympathies, Mrs Mathews."

"Thank you, Dr Patel."

She remained frozen to the tarmac, her mobile still pressed to her ear, eyes streaming. The bag piled high with sugary and salty snacks slipped from her fingers as a wave of excruciating pain and remorse crashed over her body. She crumpled forward, clutching her stomach, her breath lost—bile rising.

"Are you okay, dear?" An elderly couple tottered toward her, their wrinkled faces expressing concern. The man bent to collect the contents of her fallen bag and the woman grasped her arm, supporting her.

"Are you pregnant, dear? The exhaustion can just sneak up on you, can't it? Which one is your car?"

Rebecca numbly pointed to her silver car. They shuffled to it, helping her open the driver's door, and lowering her gently into the seat.

"Can we fetch you some coffee or a bottle of sparkling water? I know I went right off coffee when I was expecting our Lorraine, didn't I, Archie, and drank gallons of sparkling water. Maybe you're having a little girl, too, love?" She patted the still silent Rebecca's hand.

"No, thank you," she croaked, anxious for them to leave, feeling her emotions thaw just enough for realisation to dawn and urgency to kick in. She needed to hare back up to Newcastle.

[153]

When Claudia asked later how she'd driven back to Newcastle after such an immeasurable shock, she was unable to recall any aspect of that nightmare journey, grateful it had become so familiar she didn't need to engage her brain. Her thoughts had no room for anything other than her father and the enormous gaping hole his passing would leave in her life.

As she dashed into the reception area of the Freeman Hospital, she caught sight of Claudia and Paul loitering anxiously at the coffee vending machine and blessed them with all her aching heart. At last, she allowed her tears to flow freely, the self-restraint required for the drive broke as they took turns drawing her into their arms and fetching cups of appalling sludge labelled coffee for her whilst they waited for Doctor Patel to arrive.

"The hospital contacted us, too. Had our home number," Claudia explained. "We wanted to be here with you. How you managed that drive, Becky, I'll never know." She added, "The kids are fine. My sister's staying over with them."

As time crawled by, darkness pressed against the hospital windows. The muted TV monitor flashed disjointed pictures as they waited, cloaked in sadness. Doctor Patel eventually arrived, directing them into a cold, sterile side room lit by the ubiquitous neon strip lights. Rebecca shuddered. If these walls could talk, what a horrific story they would tell. She doubted anything happy ever happened in this room.

She sat, sandwiched between Claudia and Paul, nodding numbly, agreeing, thanking, understanding, but nothing penetrated her pain. Paul grasped her clammy hand, assuming the lead until the doctor excused himself to resume his treatment of the living.

"I wasn't there for him, Claudie." Rebecca wept. "I so wanted to be with him at the end, not for him to die alone! The call came in the Motorway Services car park in Wetherby. I should have been at

[154]

his bedside or at home with you, instead of haring back to my life in London. I'm a hateful daughter." Her body convulsed with heaving sobs.

"Becky, wherever you were you couldn't have changed what happened. George was very ill, you know that. He wasn't aware of where he was or who sat in vigil at his bedside. He's at peace now, darling. He's with Marianne, whom he missed every single day—more so toward the end. He reminisced endlessly to me and Daisy about your mum. Stop berating yourself. It serves no purpose."

Claudia stroked Rebecca's hair, the rhythmic motion bringing calm to her ragged senses. "Come on. Nothing more we can do here. Let's get you home. There're phone calls to make," Paul said.

"Oh, gosh yes, I've got to call Bradley. I think he may be in Paris. And Lucinda. I don't think I have the strength to face it all."

CHAPTER TWENTY-FIVE

"BRADLEY, IT'S REBECCA." Her voice quivered with grief, but her stomach churned at having to interrupt his weekend jaunt. She could predict his immediate reaction to her call.

"Rebecca? Me and Cheryl are in Paris. Can this wait?"

"No, Bradley, it can't wait. I'm ringing to let you know that Dad passed away last night. He suffered a stroke last Friday and never regained consciousness. The funeral is on Monday. Will you come up to Newcastle? Claudia and Paul have offered you a bed. I'll stay at the cottage."

"I'm sorry to hear about George, Rebecca. I really am. He was a decent father-in-law. But we don't get back from Paris until tomorrow evening. I haven't told you, but I've got an interview next Tuesday for a position with an international law firm in Dubai! It's a fantastic opportunity, Rebecca. I can't mess this up. I need to cram up before the interview. I don't want to be exhausted from a grueling trip up to Northumberland the day before."

"Bradley, my father has died. Are you telling me you're not attending his funeral? Not coming to pay your respects?" Bradley had a knack for astonishing her, but this was beyond belief.

"Rebecca, I can't miss this life-changing opportunity. Got to chase the cash. The interview is Tuesday and then the four best candidates are being flown out to Dubai—first class of course—for the final selection process and to meet the directors. Even if I don't get the job, it'll be a free jaunt for me and Cheryl."

She was astounded. How could she have been married to this guy? Had he always been such a heartless human being? Yes, she concluded, he had no redeeming features she could recall.

"Well, the funeral is at two p.m. at Matfen Church, then on to the crem and back to Claudia and Paul's for a drink. Max would love to see you. He's lost his granddad, don't give him cause to think he's lost his father, too."

She slowly dropped the receiver into its cradle.

"HELLO, LUCINDA. IT'S Rebecca."

"Oh, yes, Rebecca. Where are you? I note you're not at your desk. I was expecting you back this morning. I take a dim view of your continued absence after I generously allowed you two extra days leave. I must raise the Exquisite Forest case with you. Because you were unable to make the appointment on Monday, it seems we have lost Mrs Russell's business. She refused to allow me to conduct the purchase—"

"Could I interrupt for a moment, Lucinda?"

A distinct sharp intake of breath could be heard down the line, but she didn't possess the courage for another confrontation. "My father passed away last night. I was on my way back to London when I received the telephone call from the hospital. I've returned

[157]

to organise the funeral arrangements. It's scheduled for next Monday. I will be back in the office on the following Wednesday." She had never dared being so assertive with Lucinda before, but her bravery had the desired effect.

"Please, accept my sympathies, Rebecca. I understand how difficult it is. I hope the funeral is cathartic. I will inform John Baringer of your loss. We will expect you back at your desk the following Monday, ninth of September."

"Thanks, Lucinda." Tears rolled down her cheeks at the other woman's brusque and totally unexpected kindness. Lucinda has obviously lost someone close to her.

"HI, DEB, IT'S Becky. Before Lucinda announces the news to everyone, I wanted to tell you my dad passed away last night. The funeral's on Monday. I've got lots to sort out up here, won't be back until the Monday after. Claudia and Paul are here supporting me."

"Oh, Becky, I'm so sorry. Poor you, how are you holding up? Can I help with anything? Me and Fergus will drive up to Northumberland at the weekend to be with you."

"Thanks, Deb, but there's no need to come to Northumberland. Don't know what Lucinda would say if half the office staff were absent!"

"Blast Lucinda!" And then she burst into noisy tears.

Rebecca had never heard Deb swear before. She was touched by her distress. "Deb, will you tell Nathan and Georgina for me? I can't bear to make any more calls."

"Course I will." She sniffed. "Sorry for the tears. Don't worry about a thing this end. Me and Nathan, and probably Georgina, will keep on top of your workload so you don't have piles of work to come back to. Got nothing else to do any way!"

Rebecca wondered what she meant. Then she remembered Nathan's court hearing at the Family Proceedings court had been the previous day. "I feel guilty about letting Nathan down. How did the hearing go?"

A comical trumpet noise rattled down the phone line, followed by a ragged inhale of breath, causing Rebecca to smile for the first time in the last week. Deb could lift even the darkest of moods.

"He went, Becky. Emma attended, too—no lawyers. Neither of them can afford it. The court ordered welfare reports to be prepared, but they succeeded in having a civilised discussion in front of a mediator and he's hopeful of an agreement. But the summer holidays are nearly over, so Millie will be back at school on Monday. A trip up to Edinburgh isn't looking likely. There's something going on with Nathan, but he won't budge under even the toughest of cross-examination.

"Oh, and Lucinda's been invited to her sister's wedding in Palma next weekend, so she won't be in the office—a week of blessed relief!"

"Okay, Deb, thanks."

"We're all thinking of you, Becky. I'm so sorry." And, as she depressed the call button, she burst into tears again.

Nathan scooted his chair over to Deb's desk and patted her hand awkwardly. Deb rarely gave into tears. "Come on, Deb. You'll sort this out. It's not the end of the world, you know."

"I know, I know. And that was Becky on the phone. Her father passed away last night. She's devastated. Funeral's on Monday. She's not back until the Monday after. Lucinda gave her another week off. That's amazingly out of character, but it'll be because she's gallivanting off to that gorgeous wedding in Palma, the jammy cow! Oh, Nathan, what are we going to do?" Her ample bosom heaved.

"Put it into perspective, I'd say, Deb. Poor Becky, look what she has to organise now—her beloved father's funeral. In only five days. Maybe I'll be forced to do something similar in the next couple months. You only get a week to organise everything."

Deb wailed.

"What I mean is, you've got a joyous celebration to organise and you've still got eight weeks! I know you've been planning the dream fairy tale wedding at Radley Hall for the last century and what has happened is horrendous, but it's not the end of the world. It doesn't mean you can't marry Fergus—which is the intended conclusion anyway—just that you can't have the expensive, over-elaborate reception at Radley Hall. Let's think out of the box!"

Shocked at the positivity from Nathan, Deb dried her tears and stared at him. "Who are you? And what have you done with my friend, Nathan Derek Atkins? You're the deliverer of doom and gloom. Not the provider of positive alternative solutions!"

"What I mean is," said Nathan, ignoring her jibe, "St Aiden's Church has a church hall. Go and visit the Reverend Briggs, explain what happened, and hire the village hall. I know, I know, not in the same league as Radley Hall. No stunning photos in the rambling grounds. No gourmet food served in minute morsels of delight. No long-legged beauties offering cool, sparkling Bolly, but I won't hold that against you!

"What I'm saying is don't cancel the wedding. You've still got Fergus, you've still got the church, you've still got the fabulous honeymoon Fergus has promised to arrange. Me, Becky, and loads of others will rally 'round—smarten up St Aiden's church hall with whatever theme you want. Becky could probably do with something to keep herself busy, take her mind off losing her dad. It might work."

This was the most optimistic speech Deb had ever heard Nathan make. She allowed her distressed mind to meander through his proposal. It was an option. She was still devastated that a kitchen blaze at Radley Hall had discarded her long-awaited fairy tale wedding with a bonfire, sending her dreams up in flames, but everything Nathan had said was true. She still had Fergus, she still had eight weeks, and she had an army of family and friends who would rally around to salvage the party of the decade.

"You are an absolute star, Nathan Atkins. I love you!" She flung her chubby arms around him—his head at the perfect height to bury his nose into the crease of her breasts—just as Lucinda appeared at the office door to deliver the sad announcement about Rebecca's father.

CHAPTER TWENTY-SIX

FUNERAL DAY, MONDAY, second of September—her father's seventy-fourth birthday. Rebecca hoped he was celebrating over a glass of Dom Perignon's best vintage with Marianne.

The promised Indian summer had materialised. The warm, sunny morning and the four drops of herbal Rescue Remedy, forced on her by Claudia, were producing a welcome blanket of calmness. Seventy-four was not old in the grand scheme of things, but it wasn't youthful either. George had enjoyed a fulfilled life—a strong, loyal, and loving marriage to Marianne, and a grandson whom he adored. She wouldn't count herself in the list of George's successes yet. She had failed her father on a number of levels, but not on the love and affection scale. She had adored him and her mum.

Rebecca had agonised over whether Max should be allowed to attend the funeral, but led by Claudia, she accepted it would be too distressing to witness the exit of his beloved granddad in a coffin. A promised trip to the cinema was more appropriate to a four year old's wellbeing.

Claudia's sister, Alison, had leapt at the chance to indulge in child-friendly activities on the last day of their summer holidays. School resumed tomorrow for Rowan and Harry, and even Daisy was excited about starting playgroup. School would start on Wednesday for Max. Rebecca was grateful for the extra days Lucinda had surprisingly offered. She could drop him at the school gates, be around to settle him in for his first few days, and meet him again at the end of the day, a rare treat. It had been a high price to pay for the privilege though.

She surveyed the tiny Victorian church. Her mum and dad had been married there, she had been christened there, and Marianne had hoped one day to attend her only daughter's wedding within its quaint stone walls. Bradley had refused, of course. Said holding their wedding there would be hypocritical, as neither of them attended church in London. Rebecca would have adored to have kept up the family tradition and been married at Holy Trinity, with its bells ringing in the tower proclaiming their happiness, flowers arranged by the village ladies, walking in a winding procession to the church from her childhood home. The photographs would have been so pretty.

But, of course, Bradley's views had prevailed and they were married at Chelsea Register Office in a non-descript, impersonal room with no windows, on a rainy Thursday in June, photographs snapped on the ugly stone steps outside. They then immediately departed for Heathrow and their honeymoon in New York, when she would have preferred a reception for friends and family, and a sun-drenched tropical beach with swinging, hammocks, and palms trees.

She clenched her shoulders, straightening her spine in preparation for the onslaught of pain as the organ music increased its volume, signaling the arrival of her dad's coffin at the heavy arched door of the church. Claudia and Paul grasped Rebecca's cold, clammy hands as the congregation stood to await his arrival.

The somber congregation swelled the little church to its limit. George had been a keen member of the local Rotary Club and a regular at the village pub, The Black Bull, his familiar pipe clenched between his teeth—his dummy, her mum used to call it. Even some of her mum's old friends attended, offering their condolences and paying their respects. He had been well-loved and for that Rebecca was grateful.

Realisation dawned. George was forever drumming this into Rebecca's stubborn psyche—how important a stable family and a supportive community were for Max.

She turned slightly as the coffin was lowered in front of her. She was shocked but touched to meet Josh's eyes. He and his father stood erect, green tweed caps in hand at the back of the church, proof the village grapevine was alive and well. She received a sympathetic nod and smile, which she tried to return but she suspected hers was more akin to a grimace.

She spotted Jean Peters from St Oswald's Lodge, who had been very kind, helping her to sort through her father's few personal items. She'd sent a welcome arrangement of baby-blue hydrangea from the care home garden, which, she'd reported proudly, the residents had selected and arranged themselves for George.

How Rebecca endured the service, she had no idea. When she tried to dredge the details from her memory later, she drew a blank. She had, however, been reliably informed by those friends of her mum, who held great stock in a well-delivered funeral homily, that it had been moving, personal, and Reverend Andrews had excelled himself, being well acquainted with George's life achievements.

Claudia and Paul provided an essential prop for Rebecca in the church. She felt isolated, despite the packed congregation and the outpouring of compassion for her loss. In the back of the shiny, black limousine on the way to the crematorium, they buttressed her flagging spirits, assuaged her fear that she might collapse as she uttered her final farewell to her beloved dad and the red velvet curtains drew around his coffin.

They flanked her like sentries at the crematorium's oak door, Claudia grasping her elbow as she thanked everyone for their kindness and attendance at the worst kind of celebration—that of a life lost.

Shaking each proffered hand, she accepted their sympathetic utterings with a tight smile, knowing she would never have cause to see these people again and for some reason that saddened her deeply. These mourners had been an integral part of George and Marianne's life, their extended, caring community—something Rebecca would never experience in Hammersmith, unless she counted Brian, and she'd rather not.

A titanic silver tureen of homemade pea and ham soup— George's favourite and a local delicacy—and a mountain of sandwiches provided by Claudia's mother, Margaret, was the awaiting, comforting sight in Claudia's chaotic kitchen. The French doors, arms peeled back, welcomed guests into the warm, sunny garden as Claudia's loving home started to spin its magic on Rebecca's flattened spirits.

Her mood lifted further under the onslaught of the exuberance of the children returning from their expedition to the cinema. The sandwich mountain was scaled and reduced to crumbs.

Max glued himself to Rebecca's side, refusing to let her out of his sight. Rebecca knew he feared her disappearance from his life like his granddad, like his father. With constant and loving reassurance over the days since her father's passing, she'd calmed his anxiety, but with so much trauma to deal with over the last few weeks, it wasn't surprising he was distressed.

It had been painful to watch the relief spread across his freckled face of not having to return to Tumble Teds and see Stanley, his mortal enemy, ever again. But starting school held fresh fear and trepidation of the unknown.

If only Bradley had had the decency to simply take Max out for the day, away from witnessing the trauma of those adults closest to him. Max had queried why his dad hadn't come to visit when granddad was ill or to the funeral, but she suspected the answers she had uttered had not satisfied him. She wanted to wrap him in her arms, to insulate him from this continued pain and confusion.

Last night, for the first time in weeks, she had extracted her Little Green Book from its resting place at the bottom of her satchel, craving its guidance and straightforward advice. She hadn't expected miracles, but turning its emerald face over in her hand the book felt like a familiar, comforting friend as she commenced the nightly battle with the sleep-deprivation demon.

She'd parted the pages at the section heading 'Wishes with Children', running her weary eyes down the list of activities its wisdom covered. It served to remind her that life was short and children grew into adults so fast that each milestone should be treasured. That time spent baking, gluing, painting, constructing dens from clothes driers were cherished moments that remained wrapped in memory for the rest of one's life. These were the prized experiences her father had reminisced about with her during his remaining days, not the endless hours she'd slaved at university or at work.

Building these dreams for Max was all she had left to achieve now, as her dad had persisted in reminding her, even on the final day she had spent in his company. Her silent promise to her father was made as tears coursed down her face. She would spend the rest of her life, be it long or be it short, living up to his and her mother's example.

"*Strive to make time in your day to enjoy the small things together with your child. Share a book, play a board game, craft a paper aeroplane, attempt a new sport, visit a museum, but above all, step off the daily treadmill and just take pleasure in each other's company,*" the pages declared. "*These are the unforgettable memories we lay down for the future.*" The book once again had solidified its words of wisdom in her befuddled mind. She'd understood them already, but they served as a timely reminder.

She vowed to live by these rules from now on, in memory of George Arthur Phillips, born September second, 1937. Beloved husband of Marianne Louise, adored father of Rebecca Jane, and treasured granddad to Max Bradley. R.I.P.

CHAPTER TWENTY-SEVEN

"WHERE'S NATHAN ANYWAY?" Rebecca asked Deb, noticing his unusually tidy cubicle was devoid of his spiky hair and flicking pen.

The whole September morning was spent embroidering the trials and tribulations of the eventful previous weeks. High Court proceedings had claimed Lucinda's presence—her first day back after her week's leave attending her sister's wedding in Palma. So, whilst the cat was away, the mice gossiped.

First Rebecca recounted the tragedy of the last two weeks, her strength and fortitude building as each dreadful detail was expelled from the heavy weight in her chest into Deb's listening ear.

Then it was Deb's turn to relive the nightmare of the telephone call with the bombshell news that the kitchen at Radley Hall had been razed to the ground by a fierce electrical fire. Fortunately, no one had been injured, but there was no possibility they could honour their commitment to hold her wedding reception at Radley

Hall on the thirty first of October. However, any date next March would be fine, if she cared to reschedule.

Rebecca was upset she hadn't been around to help Deb through this, confirming to her once again her failure to be available for anyone who needed her. Deb had expressed her regret for not making the journey to Northumberland to provide support for Rebecca, but they both agreed the timing of tragedies couldn't be predicted or manipulated to fall neatly whenever a window of availability opened.

Deb shared the current tentative plan, still in its infancy, to hold the reception in the St Aiden's church hall, but not the intricate details as she had loads more gossip to update Rebecca with.

"You're not going to believe this, Becky. We didn't want to bother you with any of this, you know—my wedding disaster, Nathan's contact problems, Lucinda's wedding invitation, Georgina's news—because of the terrible time you were going through, you had enough on your plate. But I've just got to spill!

"Nathan's in Edinburgh! With Millie!" Her smile was filled with satisfaction as if she'd been waiting for Rebecca's surprise. "Back tomorrow. Emma even agreed to allow her to miss a day of school. They've been up there since Saturday. Gosh, where do I start?" Deb bounced in her chair with excitement, revealing the fact that she had dropped at least eight pounds since Rebecca had been away.

"Well start, come on." Rebecca welcomed the diversionary gossip as she struggled to concentrate on tackling the backlog of work piled high on her cluttered grey desk.

"Nathan's a secret member of F4J!" Deb blurted. "You know, *Fathers for Justice*? He was arrested when you were in Northumberland for scaling the Tower Bridge in his wizard's costume, flying the flag for father's rights!" She giggled, flicking her long, rippling waves behind her cute ears, her breasts quivering as she swung to and fro on her swivel chair, animated by the riveting story of Nathan's bravery, or stupidity!

"Are you're joking? I saw that piece on the news when I was at Claudia's. That was Nathan? Wow, I said to Claudia I sympathised with the poor guy for taking the fight into his own hands. But Nathan? Arrested?"

"Yep. Cautioned and released. Kept it quiet at work though— he's terrified of the reaction of Lucinda and John Baringer. Afraid he'll be fired on the spot, which, I have to say, is a possibility. However, he's been in such demand from the media since the stunt that a long and lucrative career in television beckons. You'll never believe this, but he's been invited onto *This Morning* next week to talk about lobbying Parliament on fathers' and grandparents' contact rights, a subject he's ideally placed to publicise."

"But that stunt could have scuppered his chances at the court hearing, Deb! Emma handed the perfect excuse to continue her refusal of contact with Millie, 'a father so irresponsible as to scale an iconic monument cannot be trusted with the care of a vulnerable child' argument! Poor Nathan, he must have been desperate to pull such a stunt."

But Deb didn't look at all sympathetic or concerned about Nathan's predicament, so Rebecca knew there was more to the story. She scooted her chair closer to Deb's as she continued with the intriguing tale.

"You would have thought so, wouldn't you? But no, Becky. Oh ye of little faith, as Nathan himself would say. Emma saw the item on the news, too, says she recognised Nathan. She contacted him the next day after he'd been released from police custody. Nathan was totally expecting a hurl of abuse, but get this, she told him how brave she thought he was, how impressed she'd been with his courage to scale the heights of Tower Bridge. She offered to meet him for coffee for him to spill all the details the next day after work and to discuss progressing contact because Millie now thought her dad was a real life wizard!"

"No!" Rebecca giggled.

"Well, look at his hair, there is a similarity to the most famous wizard of our time! Anyway, it went so well he plucked up the courage to enquire about a trip to Edinburgh. To say he's overjoyed is an understatement. He's so grateful to you for sharing the advice of the little green book. Remember? We teased him about his procrastination habit? And persuaded him take the first step to issue those court proceedings, instilling in him the confidence to make changes in his life and seek out his heart's desire. Look how the book's pearls of wisdom have changed you over the last six months!

"But most of all, he's ecstatic his mother will get to see Millie before it's too late. He's hopeful Emma and he can agree to contact every other weekend, and so far, Emma is amenable. She's enjoying being a part of his minor celebrity status, I think. He says he's hung up his wizard's robes for good!"

"Good grief, I'm stunned. I'm so relieved Emma saw sense and did the right thing. It's time I did the same."

"What do you mean?" Deb asked sharply.

She was prevented from answering the searching question in Deb's eyes as Lucinda strode into their office. Deb scattered back to her desk, but then performed an almost theatrical double take.

Lucinda appeared in their room clad in a gorgeous cream Italian designer suit—slim, pencil-straight skirt, short-fitted, single-breasted jacket with a pale rose shirt, cuffs peeping from her sleeves, manicured hands clutching a pile of files topped by a pink-ribboned brief, and bronzed from her recent trip to Palma. Her hair radiated golden highlights from the sun or a treatment, Rebecca wasn't sure which. But the most surprising thing of all was that she was smiling!

Deb looked positively terrified.

"May I first of all say, Rebecca, how saddened I am about your father's passing? I hope the funeral went as smoothly as we can expect these occasions to go in the circumstances. Secondly, I have just completed my longest-running court case, the Barton Sapphire case, which has been on-going for five long years. Our clients were successful and have been awarded five hundred thousand pounds in legal costs."

"Thank you, Lucinda, I'm grateful for the time you allowed me to organise everything in Northumberland." Rebecca felt braver now she had made her decision, so she added, "You look, erm, different?"

"Yes, sick of all the black. A change is called for." And she swiveled on her red, four-inch stiletto heels, leaving an aroma of spring flowers in her wake.

"What the..." said Deb, winding in her jaw.

Deb glanced across the office and saw Georgina smirking. "You know something, don't you? Spit it out. I can tell you're bursting!"

Georgina flicked her short ebony curls behind her ears. "I've been bursting to spill the details I heard in the boardroom this morning from Grace. She got it straight from John Baringer himself.

"Lucinda just got back from Palma last night," Georgina whispered, glancing over her shoulder as though making sure Lucinda had disappeared into her corner office. She grabbed Nathan's empty chair and scuttled over to Rebecca and Deb. "Attended her sister's wedding. Her younger sister, Louise, lives in Majorca. Married a Majorcan guy—gorgeous, looks like one of those passionate bull fighters, smoldering Mediterranean good looks, sun-kissed skin, taut buttocks, firm abs—"

"Calm down, Georgina, you're dribbling. Get on with the gossip!" Deb was leaning in so close, her breasts threatened to spill from her low-cut, emerald silk blouse.

"She raised her sister, did you know? Their mother died when Lucinda was fifteen, Louise only seven, weeks before Lucinda sat her GCSEs. Instead of celebrations and parties after the exams, Lucinda stayed home, caring for Louise so their father could continue working and keep the roof over their heads. She studied hard for her A levels. What else was there for her to do, with a nine year old to nurture? She chose the local uni, too, instead of taking up the place she was offered to read law at Cambridge. Her sister would only have been ten or eleven by then. Their father died when Louise was at Leicester Uni studying modern languages. Lucinda was able to relocate to London to pursue her own belated dream of become a partner in a top London City law firm. Louise graduated ten years ago, landing a job in an infants' school in Palma, which she loved. Can't say I blame her when you see the guys on offer there. Look at Raphael Nadal and Sergio Garcia!

"Anyway, that left Lucinda with no family, no friends, and no boyfriend. So she did what she had always done and immersed herself in her glittering career, achieving her dream by becoming the youngest female partner here at Baringer, as we all know!"

"But I don't understand her sudden change in fashion choices, Georgina. Those stilettos are gorgeous, Spanish designer definitely, but they're scarlet. For the office! And did she say she's just come from one of the most important court cases of her career?" Rebecca was flabbergasted.

"I haven't got to the punch line yet—the girl-gets-the-guy bit!" Georgina continued, retucking her curls behind her ears. "Her sister's wedding to the fiery Spaniard was held in the gothic splendor of La Seu Cathedral in Palma the weekend before last. Lucinda spent the following week of her annual leave holidaying in Majorca, sampling the local offerings." She raised her darkly arched eyebrows as if aware of their undivided attention.

"She vacationed on an eighty foot luxury yacht berthed in Palma Marina with Raphael, the best man!"

"Wow," Deb mouthed, eyes fixed on Georgina.

"No prizes for guessing how he succeeded in melting the ice dragon's heart! The rhythm of the Mediterranean waves crashing against the quay, gently rocking the sparkling white yacht, whilst the passionate young—well, youngish—Spaniard launched his scorching breath onto the frozen dragon's melting desire, their building passion, their mutual—"

"Georgina, what's the matter with you? Is Jonathan not stepping up to the mark in the bedroom department or something?" Deb smirked.

"Oh, no complaints there," she replied with a glint in her eye. "Did you see her suit? It's silk, must have cost a thousand euros. Raphael clearly indulged her shopping craving in Palma, and that's why she's showing it off. But that's not all.

"Lucinda was livid when we lost the Exquisite Forest business." She nodded at Rebecca. "Yes, haven't told you, and you probably haven't spoken to Sam Russell, what with everything that's happened, Becky, but Sam turned up at the office for her appointment with you. Lucinda had decided to conduct the interview herself rather than postpone what she hoped would be a lucrative business relationship. As usual, Lucinda was less than sympathetic to your predicament in Northumberland, so Sam refused to do business with her. Were you aware of Exquisite Forest's ethical trading policies?

[174]

"Well, Lucinda was furious you hadn't warned her in advance. Thankfully, you didn't come back on that Wednesday—oh, no! I'm so sorry…I didn't think…" Georgina's face fell.

"It's okay, Georgina. So the sudden transformation, from being livid beyond coherence to floating around in a cloud of fresh apple blossoms, dressed from the pages of a high-end glossy fashion magazine, is attributed to one sultry week of passion with a Spanish guy with a yacht and buttocks of steel to die for?" Rebecca queried, her eyebrows raised in skepticism.

"I've seen the wedding photos—he's dazzlingly handsome." She spoke as if to a very stupid child. "He's a *multi-millionaire,* with an *eighty-foot* yacht moored in Palma Marina, one of the prettiest in the Mediterranean. What's not to like? But the boat's not the reason for the Cheshire cat smile. That cat got the cream, over and over."

Deb snorted. "Let's hope it's the start of a Spanish odyssey. I'm inviting them to the wedding. Shame he won't be able to land his helicopter on the grounds of Radley Hall! Becky, bring Max as your plus one, won't you?"

"He started school last Wednesday. He's regressed to his stressed-out, anxious self, chewing his new school jumper sleeve, flinching at the sight of any domestic pet. He's latched on to Erin, you know, Brian's daughter, but I'm really worried about him, he's so listless. Every day last week when I collected him from the school gates he said he hated it and asked when we were going to live in Northumberland."

"Are you considering jumping ship?"

"Yes."

CHAPTER TWENTY-EIGHT

"HI, BECKY. SORRY about your dad. Tough call." Nathan bounced to his cubicle and pinged on his computer, but his pale face spoke of his concern and empathy for his friend and colleague's bereavement. He flashed his dark eyes and a smile across the office to Deb, followed by a nod of acknowledgement to Georgina, who was wrestling with a difficult client call.

"Thanks, Nathan. I'm doing okay," Rebecca replied. "But what about you? I'm delighted to hear your news. How was the trip to Edinburgh with Millie? How's your mum?"

"Becky, it was awesome. Mam and Millie spent the whole time in Mam's back garden. Mam was able to sit in her wheelchair wrapped up in her fleece blanket on the patio, the heater blasting—she gets so cold now—and Millie just raced around the garden, spotting all the plants and flowers, trees, birds, and butterflies. Mam showed her sketches and watercolours she had painted when she was able. Emma doesn't have a garden so Millie went wild!

"We played croquet with Mam's old clubs, built a birdhouse out of the bits of wood and nails Dad keeps in the shed, and then painted it a lurid green. Enough to frighten any bird away." He smiled.

Nathan had never been so animated, so talkative, so full of joy and enthusiasm—no pen flying between his fingers.

"I'm so grateful to Emma for allowing me to take Millie up to Scotland. Mam's really frail now." He paused, flashing a concerned expression across to Deb who smiled and nodded back in encouragement.

"What I really want to do is thank you, Becky, and that little green book of miracles of yours, for giving me the shove up the backside I needed to do something positive. To take a leap forward into the unknown. Did Deb tell you about the police caution?" he asked sheepishly, keeping his voice low, so as not to disturb Georgina's phone call.

"Yes, she did. It seems to me Emma's change of heart had more to do with that ridiculous stunt than any little green book or court hearing though!"

"She admired my courage, she said." Nathan sat up proudly. "But of course there were the TV interviews and the appearance next week on 'This Morning' with Phillip Scofield to speak about fathers' rights. I'm a celebrity now, Becky! I've even had a call from the Big Brother House production company asking if I'd be interested in the next series! Emma wants me to do it, but I'm not sure."

Deb and Rebecca rolled their eyes. Whatever Emma's motivation for the renewed relationship between Millie and Nathan, it had had the desired result. It was unlikely Nathan would become a TV star, but stranger things had happened in the crazy topsy- turvy world of celebrity.

[177]

Georgina wound up her telephone conference, and then dragged her desk chair across the office to join in the team's gossip. No one seemed concerned by the possibility of Lucinda emerging from her lair and chastising them for their blatant breach of the office manual.

Nathan rummaged in his tatty rucksack. "Becky, on the way back down from Edinburgh, I picked up an *Evening Chronicle* at Newcastle Central Station. Have you seen this?" He unfolded the newspaper, smoothing back the pages until he jabbed his finger on an article he'd outlined in red.

NORTHUMBERLAND'S MORNINGSIDE TOWERS RESIDENTIAL CARE HOME SCANDAL by Anna Marie Stubbs, health and social care correspondent.

Morningside Towers Residential Care Home has failed the ultimate test of compassion in our society. Presenting to the world a luxurious façade, offering residents chiropody, hairdressing, a swimming pool, and spa facilities, even an on-site cinema for those black-and-white war movies favoured by our senior citizens, whilst behind its closed doors lay unimaginable pain and suffering for its twenty-five elderly residents, left dehydrated by the staff who failed to meet even this most basic of needs, resulting in eight people being admitted to hospital with severe dehydration.

"Older people are not always aware of becoming dehydrated," said Dr David Catchpole, Specialist Registrar in Geriatrics at the Royal Victoria Infirmary in Newcastle. "And if staff are not vigilant about ensuring residents have enough to drink each day, they can become seriously ill, like the residents at Morningside Towers. Overheated rooms are also a factor meaning the body requires more liquid."

Many older people don't receive the basic standard of care essential for their wellbeing and over the last five years more than nine hundred and fifty people have been admitted to hospital with dehydration and some two

[178]

hundred and eighty four with malnutrition, although most of these are from their own homes.

This dreadful incident at Morningside Towers is being investigated by the Care Quality Commission, but it is hoped that it will be a wake-up call for all residential care home managers to be vigilant in providing sufficient food and water, those most basic of life's requirements to their vulnerable residents who rely on them for the provision of care, sometimes at great financial expense.

"Oh, no, that was the residential care home I wanted for Dad, but couldn't afford." Rebecca's horrified eyes widened as she took in the newspaper story, her heart hammering its opposition to such barbaric treatment of the elderly and most vulnerable members of society. "I beat myself up for months about it! Oh, I'm heartbroken for the poor residents. I hope the regulator does its job properly and holds those responsible to account. No less than a criminal prosecution would satisfy me if I were a relative. "

The foursome nodded their agreement.

"It just goes to show that external presentation of beauty does not imply internal decency and goodness! Speaking of which, what's happening with Bradley?" asked Deb, as tears formed along Rebecca's auburn lashes. "What a reprobate for not attending the funeral."

"He's in Dubai. He got the job over there. He and Cheryl are sorting out a luxurious, three-bedroom apartment and 'interviewing domestic staff', to do the household chores and to drive Bradley to work and Cheryl to the shops! No mention at all about maintaining contact with Max, only the fantastic salary he will be getting, the huge bonuses on offer if he meets target, the generous share scheme for the staff, and the diamond-white Porsche he's leasing."

Rebecca inhaled a breath deep into her lungs. Now was as good a time as any to announce her decision. "I've decided to go back home—to Northumberland. I made the decision right after Dad's funeral, but now that Bradley is relocating to Dubai, it doesn't matter where Max and I live. Anyway, Emirates have direct flights from Newcastle Airport to Dubai if he wants to visit."

Her colleagues remained silent.

"Max is unhappy here in London. He'll have to endure Breakfast Club and Afterschool Club every day of his school life, which he's adamant he doesn't want to do. It's traumatised him, being the last child to be collected from nursery every day. I can't revisit that upon him at school, too. And it costs a fortune. He'd stopped his sleeve-chewing whilst we were on holiday at Rosemary Cottage—he adored the freedom, the fresh air, the lush green fields, and even the farm animals—but it has started over again now we're back in the rat race. It'll be a better life for him. You'd love the village school, Deb. It's fairy-tale perfect, and only sixty kids!"

She swung her gaze around her friends for their approval of her difficult decision. They remained mute, their jaws hanging, so she continued. "We'll live in Rosemary Cottage at first. When the probate comes through, I'll be the registered owner. Once it's sold I can pay off all my debts and the outstanding care fees to St Oswald's Lodge. Josh has offered to patch up the roof temporarily as it looks like we'll be there for the winter. Probate could take about six months.

"I'm going to volunteer my services at St Oswald one day a week whilst Max is at school. Help the residents with their meals, read the newspapers to them, walk them around the garden that Dad loved so much. Hopefully, I'll find a part-time job to keep food on the table.

"I'm handing in my resignation next Monday. I only have to give a month's notice. We'll move when Max breaks for half term."

"Not until after the wedding, I hope!" Deb exclaimed.

"I wouldn't miss it for the world, Deb," she said and burst into tears.

"COME ON, COME on. We've only got an hour. So many shoes, so little time," sighed Deb, as she dragged Rebecca into their favourite designer shoe emporium on Sloane Street. Floor-to-ceiling glass windows welcomed in bright sunlight to bounce its shafts onto the crystal-drop chandeliers and the mirrored cubes presenting each shoe as a piece of sculpture in its own right. The presentation of each handbag reached gallery standard, each surface pristine and sparkling. Rebecca adored the cool palate of deep cream, warm pinks, and peaches, and she particularly coveted the ivory, silk Louis-style armchairs they were courteously whisked and seated in by a pencil-thin assistant. Rebecca thought of Max, his sticky fingers wiggling, and heaved a sigh of relief he hadn't accompanied them.

They'd grabbed a few surreptitious minutes before their lunch break to consult the little green oracle's 'Wishes with Friends' section, sub-section 'Amassing a Designer Shoe Collection', but as they were in one of the world's leading shoe emporiums already, they had no need of any advice. Every handcrafted shoe was the epitome of quality and impeccable taste.

"Wow, these are my favourite," Rebecca exclaimed, reverently lifting an exquisite example of wedding footwear for closer inspection. "Look, Deb, ivory satin, peep-toe pumps, four-inch heel, scattered with Swarovski crystals. They really are to die for."

She stroked the shoes as if they were a beloved pet. The price tag made sure they were way outside her wildest dreams. She lingered on her inevitable next thought, but easily brushed the inclusion of the shoes on her wish list from her mind. No more list addiction for her.

[181]

"These little beauties are shouting my name, Becky," Deb said. "Ivory bridal sandals adorned with fine glitter and real French Chantilly lace, five-inch heel—stunning. They're a real work of art in my opinion. When the wedding's over, I'm going to display them in a glass case on my dressing table." She grimaced at the price tag. "Same price as a work of art!"

Deb's pretty face was wreathed in smiles as she floated back to the office clutching her bridal shoes in their beribboned pale pink box, her bank balance considerably lighter.

AS REBECCA WATCHED the office clock edge its way slowly to five o'clock—her mind more on what she would prepare for her and Max's dinner that evening than her clients' pressing legal issues— her landline buzzed.

"Rebecca Matthews, how can I help?"

"Hi, Becky, I'm so sorry to hear about your father." Sam's dulcet tones raised the corners of Rebecca's lips.

"Thanks, Sam. It's good of you to call. I got your message on my voicemail."

"I know how much your dad meant to you and Max. If there is anything Angus and I can do, please, ask. Ben and I attended the Junior Golf Academy last week. Ben hated being there without Max, so I've bought six sessions for Max. Don't say no. Ben begged. Please take them. I'd like to do this for Max."

Rebecca gulped down her raising emotions. Tears were always so close to the surface at the moment that any expression of kindness sent them falling.

"Thanks. He'd love to go. Look, Sam, can I apologise for the misunderstanding between Lucinda and your company's legal work? It was my entire fault. I should have been honest with you

[182]

both from the beginning. I should have explained your company's requirements to Lucinda, but I also should have anticipated that Baringer & Co is no different from most other London City law firms, with their lamentable lack of family friendly policies and obsession with the bottom line."

"I don't blame you in the slightest, Becky. I was horrified by her attitude despite knowing your father was so ill and how distressed you were. What kind of work would you produce, sat at your desk under such circumstances? More likely to make a negligent cock-up, if you ask me, and the consequences of that would be dire in your line of work. She and her ilk are so short-sighted. Companies with such stringent policies lose all their quality staff to more progressive firms, I've found. It's what causes me to strive even harder to make my company a shining example of twenty-first century working practices. See you next week at the golf club?"

"Yes, see you then. Thanks again, Sam. Max will be so excited when I tell him, and I have some news for you, too."

"Sounds intriguing!"

CHAPTER TWENTY-NINE

THE LAST FRIDAY of September dawned bleak and cold. London was at its most unattractive in the grey, slicing rain, its world famous architecture austere and gloomy, its inhabitants morose.

Max and Rebecca edged slowly forward in the mass exodus repeated every Friday at six, the snail's pace reduced even further by the lashing rain and the increased volume of traffic, people desperately trying to get away for the weekend to more pleasant spots. This would be the last tortuous journey she and Max would have to endure before their permanent relocation to Northumberland after Deb's wedding at the end of October.

"I'm excited about visiting Poppy and Josh, Mum. Can we go to the farm again and feed the animals?" Max had perked up as soon as he had scampered into the back seat, preferring the long, boring journey to killing time at Afterschool Club.

"Josh and his dad are busy with their farm, but we'll pop up tomorrow with some homemade scones for them, eh?"

She didn't want to intrude on the Charltons. She had no idea if Josh had a girlfriend or a partner, she'd never thought to ask, but it didn't prevent her from spending the next few minutes imagining what the person would be like. Would she be dark-haired or fair? A sophisticated, glamorous city lover or a country girl? Had he known her since childhood or was she someone he had met at college? She pondered on the reasons why she should find her contemplation of Josh's fictional relationships so uncomfortable.

"What about dog biscuits for Poppy, too?" Max broke into her reverie. "She might not like your homemade scones!" Charming honesty of children.

"Yes, no problem, we'll treat Poppy to some dog biscuits."

What a change around. Max was still wary of the dogs he encountered on their street in Hammersmith and in the park during the weekends, but had no fear of Poppy, Josh's black-and-white, trainee sheepdog.

The journey was one of the longest Rebecca had ever endured. Because of the deluge of rain, there had been a numbers of serious traffic accidents on the M1 and the A1. They'd broken the journey at the usual service station to change Max into his pjs two hours later than usual. Now they were stationary at Scotch Corner, another hour's drive from Newcastle. The rain still pelted at the window, the rhythm of the windscreen wipers lulling Max to sleep.

At last, they arrived at Rosemary Cottage. Even in the driving rain, Rebecca immediately noticed the garden's transformation. The ubiquitous weeds and impenetrable evergreen bushes had been tamed, the front garden, a reproduction of chocolate-box perfection, reflected in the silvery glow of the full moon. It was how she had encountered Rosemary Cottage when she first viewed it and been drawn under its mesmerising spell.

[185]

As she pushed open the paint-blistered door, dumping her old, brown leather holdall onto the parquet flooring of the hall, the cottage felt warm and inviting. She rushed back into the rain to collect a still-sleeping Max in her arms, depositing him gently on the fern-green chintz sofa, covered him with the matching mohair blanket, tucking in the sides, and planting a kiss on his sleeping face.

She opened the door of the kitchen and the rosy warmth seeped into her aching limbs. The Aga was lit! She spotted a card propped against the pale blue and white milk jug containing sprigs of freshly cut rosemary, its scent delicately fragrancing the air. She pulled the card from the thick cream envelope knowing instantly who had orchestrated such a warm welcome.

Claudia told me you'd be here this weekend with Max. Hope you're not too irritated about the garden. Me and two mates from the rugby club enjoyed the hard graft and several gallons of Guinness last Saturday. It's exactly how Mum used to do it! Dad still had a key—didn't mean to trespass on your privacy—just lit the Aga. Regards,

Josh.

XXX

His handwriting was large and bold, printed and clear. Three kisses!

The cottage wrapped its warm arms around Rebecca and Max as they snuggled together on the soft sofa eternally grateful for the kindness of friends and neighbours—the community her father had spoken so eloquently about.

"ANYONE HOME?" THE question was launched from the garden below Rebecca's bedroom window, accompanied by a welcoming corresponding bark from Poppy.

Smiling then waving, Rebecca tightened her fluffy ivory velvet robe around her narrow waist. Her body and her head ached from the long drive north hunched over the car steering wheel, her eyes screwed in high concentration, wipers flashing across her vision.

She dressed quickly before scampering down the stairs to drag open the heavy oak door.

Joshua stared at the transformed Rebecca for a few moments as he struggled to find his voice. She lifted her tumbling auburn curls from her face, cheeks blushed pink with pleasure, looking relaxed in her faded jeans and emerald cardigan. "Just called to make sure you're okay about the garden. Seemed like a good idea at the time, but now I realise it is a bit of an intrusion into your privacy." He twisted his tweed cap in his large farmer's hands.

"The garden's stunning, Josh, exactly as it was when I first viewed the cottage. Thank you so much." Rebecca beamed as she swung her eyes around the pretty cottage garden. "You and your friends must have slaved all weekend. It was such a jungle. I can see all the botanical gems that were buried under those weeds. Max and I intend to repay you with a mound of homemade scones and a box of dog biscuits. Come in for a coffee?"

She followed Josh's sapphire-blue eyes as he glanced at her attire and added, "Dreadful journey up here last night in the lashing rain. Didn't arrive until two this morning. Max is still zonked."

"Tea for me, if you have it," he suggested, settling his huge frame at the kitchen table, his cheeks reddening as he moved the jug containing the sprigs of rosemary out of his direct line of sight. Poppy made a beeline for the warmest place in the cottage next to the still-warm Aga, grunting with satisfaction.

"Josh! Yes! Can we come and visit the animals at the farm? Now?" Max bounded in. Their voices must have woken him.

"Not yet, Max sweetheart. Breakfast first. Porridge?"

"Yak, no. Chocolate Krispies!"

"Okay." She laughed, pouring two mugs of dark, steaming tea from the big green teapot and then preparing Max's breakfast.

"I've got a proposition to make, Becky."

Why did her heart flutter suddenly? What did that mean? She stood with her back to him, milk poised over the cereal bowl.

"There's no pressure, say no if you want, but think about it first. Remember I told you Dad had got planning permission to build four houses over in the lower field and to convert two of the old barns? Well, the two barns are almost completed now—just about to market them in fact. I wonder if I could engage your services with the interior design side of things? I think it would give them an edge, suggesting to potential buyers how they could look. It's a tough market out there, as you are aware, a bit more than a slop of magnolia paint is called for."

Rebecca watched as Josh fiddled with the herbs in the vase on the kitchen table as he spoke, unable to meet her gaze, the waft of sweet rosemary floating up to tickle her nostrils.

"I'm not instructing that conniving idiot Jeremy Goldacre to conduct the sale. He's been 'round to see Dad, mentioning Dad's friendship with Geoffrey Goldacre, and that he expects we'll be using their services when they are ready to market. Dad deflected the decision, but I'm adamant, Becky. Chap's dishonourable and that's taboo in my book."

At last, Josh met Rebecca's eyes across the scrubbed pine table.

"What do you say? I know you're undertaking a design course in London. I'm happy for you to do it on the weekends you come up to Northumberland and Max can help, too! Can't do any worse than me and Dad." He chuckled. "Haven't got a creative bone in our bodies for the finer details. Though I have to confess, I'm thoroughly enjoying the project management side of the conversions and can't wait to get stuck in with the new builds."

"I'd love to have a go at the interior design, Josh. And I might as well tell you now. Max and I are relocating here permanently at the end of October. I've handed in my resignation at Baringer & Co—I finish in three weeks' time, just before Deb and Fergus's wedding, so Max can complete his half term. I've lots of ideas for the barns. Thanks for the opportunity." She smiled into his gentle eyes, but he looked quickly away, disappointing Rebecca.

"Phew, what a relief! We'll pay the going rate, whatever that is."

"I don't know either, but we'll work something out. I'll be a trainee like Poppy here. Are you sure you don't want to engage a professional? I will be looking for part-time work when we get settled here, so if you hear of anything, will you let me know?"

"Well, I don't usually move in the higher echelons of the legal profession, Becky. Try to stay away from solicitors, if truth be known. Sharp suits, posh words, and they cost a fortune. You wouldn't believe how much we were charged to divide the land at the lower field into the six plots, create the easements and restrictive covenants, and what have you. No disrespect, but the fees were exorbitant!"

"I won't be looking for work in the legal profession, Josh," Rebecca replied.

She glanced out the window to where Max was playing happily with his metal detector, enjoying better access to all the nooks and crannies after the overhaul. The rain had ceased and the garden was bathed in bright sunshine. She decided to come clean to Josh. If he hated her afterwards, then at least she had been honest about her chequered past and he wouldn't be wasting his time with her or labouring under any misconceptions about her legal career.

[189]

"Josh, when I bought Rosemary Cottage, I used all my savings and the majority of Dad's savings, too, from when he sold his and Mum's house before moving into the retirement flat. I wanted to keep the purchase secret from my then-husband, Bradley, so I had the deed to the cottage put in Dad's name until I could unveil the whole package—a sort of 'tah-dah' moment that would repair our ailing marriage."

Rebecca rushed on, afraid that if she paused her courage would seep from her bones and she would not arrive at the end of her confession. "I hoped we would then re-mortgage and return Dad's money in full with the interest he'd lost—a simple enough transaction. But Bradley was horrified at the very suggestion of moving to the 'back of beyond', as he called Northumberland. He refused to agree to a mortgage, I couldn't afford it on my own, and he dropped the bombshell of his affair with Cheryl at the same time".

Intermittent high-pitched beeps assured Rebecca that Max was busy with his treasure hunting activities, so she continued, her voice wavering with emotion just like the sounds of the metal detector.

"Then Dad had his stroke and needed residential care so moved to St Oswald's Lodge. I wanted him to move to Morningside Towers, more luxurious, and yes, I've heard the scandal. Further evidence of my questionable decision-making!

"As I had used all Dad's savings for the cottage, no money was available to pay for Dad's care fees, so I borrowed twenty thousand pounds from the bank and paid his fees until Christmas, hoping that in the meantime the cottage would sell. From the proceeds, I'd be able to repay the bank loan and Dad could move to Morningside Towers. But as you know the cottage didn't sell—the roof caved in, the garden became a jungle. Who would want to buy it in that state?

"Bradley refused to pay child support for Max as he never wanted children in the first place and views Max as solely my responsibility. I couldn't afford to pay back the loan to the bank, pay the rent on our flat in London, and Max's child care fees, so I fell behind with the repayments. To cut a painful story short, the bank went for bankruptcy which meant I could no longer practice as a solicitor."

Rebecca wiped away a single tear as it trickled down a well-worn path on her smooth, pale cheek. The loss of her career still lacerated her heart, but she had almost finished her story.

"Lucinda Fleming, a partner in one of the law firms I had regular contact with as an adversary in numerous litigation matters when I worked at Harvey & Co, offered me a paralegal job in April, something I have been eternally grateful to her for. I grabbed the opportunity so Max and I could remain in London, allowing him to be near his father. Not that Bradley showed any interest in having regular contact with Max and has recently relocated himself and his girlfriend, Cheryl, to Dubai. There. That's my potted history. I doubt I will ever get another job in the legal profession again, sadly."

"Becky, I had no idea." Josh reached across the table and snatched her hand with his, his floppy golden hair sticking out at all angles, horror spreading across his face. "I blame that Jeremy Goldacre! If you had been fully aware of the condition of the cottage, you may not have bought it and this nightmare would not have unfolded. No way am I agreeing to instruct his estate agency, no matter what Dad says! But Dad'll agree with me when I tell him what that money-grabbing piece of garbage did, against my express written instructions."

Rebecca squeezed his hand, grateful for the supportive words, but continued, "It wasn't Jeremy's fault, Josh. The mistakes were all my own. I would have bought Rosemary Cottage with no roof. It's the perfect replica of my childhood dream—to live in a cottage with pink and cream roses crawling around the door, overlooking lush green and yellow meadows, a couple of children running free in the garden. I was following an unattainable dream, logic left the process, and I turned it into a nightmare."

He met and held her eyes, still holding her slender pale hand between his rough palms. He opened his mouth to speak, but an excited cry from the doorway interrupted him.

"Mum, Mum, Mum. My detector is beeping. Come and see, come and see. Josh, come and see. There's treasure in our garden!"

Josh's handsome face crinkled into a gentle smile. He released Rebecca's hand, scraped back his chair, and strode to the back door. He grabbed Max's hand and was immediately dragged to the bottom of the garden where the orchard displayed fruit-laden trees—which had previously been impenetrable without a machete—and the metal detector had been discarded, emitting an unpleasant, high-pitched squeal. Max collected it, swinging it backward and forward under the Bramley apple tree amongst the fallen fruit.

"What have you found, Max? Perhaps there's a spade in the shed. Let's do some digging."

"Yes, yes, yes."

Rebecca laughed at the boys' excitement as she sauntered back to the cottage. She felt completely calm, Rosemary Cottage performing its healing magic on her damaged emotions. She grabbed a grey hoodie for Max, whom she could see from her bedroom window digging ferociously at the bottom of the garden, smearing mud on his pjs. She'd never be able to drag him away from digging a hole to get dressed.

She pottered around the kitchen, unpacking the boxes, bags, and suitcases she'd brought with her from London. Next she went to investigate the Aladdin's cave of a shed at the bottom of her garden where she unearthed several ancient wicker baskets—assuming they'd belonged to Josh's mum—then delivered a jug of ice-cold lemonade to where Max and Josh were digging for victory.

Josh paused in his toil, quenching his thirst with the cool drink. Sweat dripped from his temples, muddy finger marks streaked his cheek, whereas Max had been rolling in it, covered in muck and mud but beaming.

"Found the Crown Jewels yet, Max?" She ruffled his hair.

"No, Mum, but we've found this muddy old coin." He held out his hand where a tiny circle of metal rested in his mud-covered palm. "Josh says it could be treasure!" But he looked doubtfully at his palm. Treasure to Max was shiny and golden, and preferably pirate.

"Yes, love. It could be." She kissed the top of his head and went off to collect a wicker basket full of the sweet-smelling Bramley apples.

Rebecca paused on her way back to the cottage. She had made a decision. "Would you be free to come over for dinner this evening, Josh? Nothing elaborate, just me, and Max, and pizza. Oh, and a gigantic apple pie!" She indicated the overflowing basket on her arm.

"Mmm, pizza, my favourite! I would love to."

"Sevenish okay?"

For the first time in years Rebecca experienced the stirring of sexual interest as her eyes lingered a little longer on Josh's strong, firm buttocks, his bulging biceps displayed as he crouched to dig the garden for Max, whilst she watched from the ancient Belfast sink peeling the Bramleys. She even felt flirtatious and resolved to revisit the little emerald book of love for gems of wisdom under the 'Romancing' Section. Deb and Nathan would be proud!

CHAPTER THIRTY

THE DELICIOUS TOFFEE aroma of sweet baking apples spread through the kitchen as Rebecca scooped the apple pie from the Aga, the ancient solid fuel stove that served as both cooker and heat source for the cottage, and set it to cool on the windowsill. She'd have to rethink her whole recipe repertoire if she had to produce food using this monstrosity.

"I'm starving, Mum. When is the pizza ready? When will Josh be here?"" asked Max as he pushed Thomas along the train track snaking the kitchen floor.

"Well, could that be Poppy I hear barking?" She held up her finger and listened.

Max rushed to drag open the heavy front door and Poppy shot passed him, curling up in her usual spot on the faded green and rose rag rug in front of the Aga.

Rebecca was relieved she had made an effort with her appearance. After washing and conditioning her hair, she'd twisted in soft sponge rollers so it now tumbled down her back in neat russet waves. She'd outlined her eyes with her favourite jade liquid eyeliner, applied a flick of mascara, and a slick of apricot lip gloss.

Her emerald, sequin-embellished t-shirt complimented the wide-legged cream linen trousers which she wore barefoot—the uneven stone floors warmed by the Aga. She'd even managed to persuade Max to jump into the old, rose-pink bath with her, luxuriating together in the thick bubbles, scrubbing away the soil from their gardening adventures, and relaxing their stiff aching muscles. With his dark auburn hair spiked with a little gel and wearing his blue denim shirt, Max presented an unusually smart image. But this was the first time Rebecca had entertained a man with Max around and she wanted to keep things low key and friendly.

"Hi." As Josh materialised at the kitchen door, clutching a chilled bottle of Moet, Rebecca's heart leapt.

Gosh, he scrubs up well!

Gone was his usual attire of loose, practical jeans or faded cords, thick woolen jumpers, and ancient green wax jacket, replaced by beautifully-cut, snug-fitting black slacks, a candy pink, blue, and lemon striped cotton shirt—cuffs wound back to display tanned, muscular forearms—and soft, brown leather loafers.

As Rebecca thanked him for the champagne, meeting his baby blue eyes, she noticed with amusement that his sandy blond hair had not responded well to a comb. It was incongruous that a man who worked in fields all day long should sport surfer-dude hair.

His pose was awkward, his presence reducing the kitchen's dimensions. Rebecca unearthed two crystal flutes as Josh joined Max on the rug next to the Aga with Poppy, employing his structural engineer's skills to expand the train track, setting the engines travelling around the intricate loops with not a flicker of fear or concern from Max as Poppy sniffed at the moving trains.

Rebecca found her eyes involuntarily sought out Josh's, rotating away as a frisson of desire shot through her veins, nerves relaxing at each sip of the delicious champagne.

Max relished every mouthful of the usually forbidden pizza. Hungrily, they dug into the apple pie Rebecca was so proud of baking from the very apples grown in her garden orchard. They eased their mismatched wooden chairs back from the table, mellow from the comforting food, well deserved after the hard labour of the day. Max yawned theatrically.

"Come on, Max, time for bed. You've had an exciting day and there's another one waiting for you tomorrow. More treasure hunting."

"Look." Josh dropped the now-scrubbed Roman coin onto the table between them. "Now I've washed off the mud, Max, can you see it has an interesting depiction?"

Three heads bent together in curiosity, a clashing mix of copper, dark auburn, and sandy thatch.

"It's definitely a coin from the Roman occupation in this area." He turned the tiny bronze coin over in his huge calloused hand. "Can you see it's stamped on one side with Emperor Hadrian's head? Look Max, see his beard? He was the first Roman Emperor to wear a beard."

Rebecca smiled slightly. What was the word Nathan had used once when they had been discussing her intense dislike of beards? *Pogonophobia*. She wouldn't have fallen for Emperor Hadrian in his day.

"Do you remember me telling you Emperor Hadrian was the one who built the Wall just north of here? To keep out the marauding Scots?"

[197]

"Yes," said Max, his eyes narrowed in concentration.

"This is a bronze coin, called a *sestertius*. They made silver and gold coins, too. Quite a few of these bronze coins have been unearthed in gardens and fields around here and they are displayed at a museum at Vindolanda, just past Hexham. Would you like to visit it one day?"

"Yes, yes, yes. Can I take my coin to show them?"

"They would love to see it, Max. But what intrigues me about this particular coin is that when we look at its reverse, the striking is still very well-defined. Can you see the Emperor on a rearing horse, addressing a line of his troops ready for battle? It's as though the coin were struck yesterday, no wear at all. With your permission, Max, I would like to show your coin to my pal, Thomas Greenwood. I went to uni with him and we still play rugby together on a Sunday morning. Tom is a professor at Newcastle University, not in Roman History, I hasten to add, but he will be able to speak to one his colleagues on the history faculty, find out more about the coin's past. What do you think?"

"Okay. As long as he doesn't spend it! I'm going to keep it in my treasure box on my windowsill. It's a great coin, Josh, but it's not gold and not as good as pirate treasure." Max reluctantly got down from his chair holding Rebecca's proffered hand. "Night, Josh. Thank you for being our friend."

Rebecca couldn't have put it better herself.

Josh leapt to his feet. "I'll be off as well. Thanks for dinner…"

"Oh, stay for a coffee. I've put the pot on the Aga to brew. I'll be down in ten minutes, when I've got this little man settled." She brushed the top of Max's soft hair affectionately and Josh relaxed into his seat, twiddling the stem of the crystal flute with fingers that were meant for a tankard!

"THAT DIDN'T TAKE long. Out like a light, bless him!" Rebecca resumed her seat at the kitchen table, grateful that Max had floated off to sleep so quickly. "It's the fresh country air and excitement of the pursuit of treasure. Thanks for spending your time with us today. Max's confidence is building by the day."

"I've enjoyed the treasure hunt, too, Becky. Any excuse to revert to childhood pleasures. I'd be up that apple tree in a shot if I didn't think you'd laugh at me! Loved apple bashing when I was a kid. Mum didn't though, wasting all those delicious apples, throwing them like boulders at my mates, Tom Greenwood being one of them. Mum had a soft spot for Tom. Never got into too much trouble when he was the instigator!"

She laughed, enjoying the rush of pleasure radiating to every part of her body, feeling vibrant as a woman, not the oppressive gloom of failure as an ex-wife, an ex-solicitor, or a bereaved daughter.

As their eyes met again, she whipped up to fetch the coffee and cream, her emotions heightened by the intensity of his gaze. What would it be like to kiss his sensuous lips, run her fingers through his tufty golden hair? To experience the sensation of his huge hands rippling over her receptive body? It had been too long.

Get a grip, Rebecca!

She poured two steaming coffees, her fingers tantalisingly brushing his as she handed over the mug.

Grasping their drinks, they wandered in to the lounge and slumped into the depths of the sagging chintz sofa, but once there, awkwardness descended. It had been relaxed, cosy, homey even in the warmth of the kitchen, busily preparing food, talking to Max, his presence acting as chaperone.

Now, despite being in a more comfortable place, Rebecca experienced a shot of vulnerability. No table between them, no Max as a diversion, she was exposed. Her shoulders tightened across her neck.

Rebecca's body language must have warned Josh of her discomfort. He swallowed hard as if his mouth was dry and dashed down his coffee.

"I must make tracks back to the farm, early start tomorrow. Rugby at the Novocastrians with Tom and James—the gardening friends. Thanks again for dinner, Becky."

He stood abruptly, towering over Rebecca, who sunk low in the ancient folds of the flowery upholstery. She struggled to her feet to walk him to the door, holding his gaze a fraction too long.

She parted her lips to answer his thanks, but in an instant, he'd cupped his hand around her soft cheek, lowering his head to hers, his warm lips seeking hers. She yielded to their softness, their taste.

Rebecca sank into his embrace. The kiss was delicate, sensitive, unsure, but her body felt none of these things—she sensed its violent rush of emotion, shocked at the intensity. He combed his fingers through her tumbling hair, stroking her neck with his thumb, her follicles electrified. She reached to caress his muscular back.

They broke away, eyes locked questioningly, unsure how to progress. She felt her cheeks flush, her breath expelled in short spurts. Wow was the only word to fill her whirling mind. All the advice and wisdom from the little green book was superfluous when the spark of mutual attraction struck.

"Rebecca, you are the most beautiful woman I've met. From the first glimpse of your auburn waves whilst weeding the garden that sunny day in August, I've wanted to experience the thrill of kissing you. Now that I have, I don't want it to end." He flushed at his intimate words, but raked her face with his gaze.

Rebecca smiled. "Well, I have no objections to a rerun."

[200]

Josh pulled her body more roughly into his arms, his mouth crushing down on hers. His smooth lips gently explored her quivering ears, her neck, her hairline until her knees weakened with longing. Still kissing, they fell back down onto the sofa, sinking deep into their desire.

They broke apart, breathless, laughing, touching each other tenderly. Josh grasped her in his arms, pulled close to his hard body. She experienced a concoction of emotions—inflamed passion and sexual hunger, mixed with a feeling of safety, of trust, knowledge there would be no pressure to move their relationship more swiftly than she wanted. She had Max to consider in every decision she made, and she had the oncoming upheaval in her life as she relocated to the north east. It wouldn't be wise to complicate or add to her pressures.

He pulled away, holding her at arm's length facing him, his eyes feasting on her glorious glow. "Becky, I'll go now, but could we spend some time together tomorrow, before you return to the mad metropolis? I did promise Max we'd finish the metal detecting and digging. And if you'll let me, I'll collect those apples for a pie for Dad."

She smiled gratefully for the option he had given her. Her preferred choice was for him to stay longer, but now wasn't the right time. She wanted to savour these new feelings before moving into a more intimate relationship. She needed to be sure, not only for her own, but for Max's sake. He didn't deserve another man leaving their lives, stealing their happiness away.

She walked Josh to the door. "We'd love to see you tomorrow. Thank Tom and James for their hard work in the garden. Maybe I can repay them when I get settled here, invite them and their partners for a barbeque and a few beers?"

[201]

"You'll need a full keg to keep those guys happy, but sounds great! Night, Becky." His lips lingered on hers in another kiss before he strode away down the newly cleared garden path, Poppy jogging along behind him.

MAX AND REBECCA took their time surfacing the next morning, luxuriating in not having to be up with the birdsong.

"Are Josh and Poppy coming today, Mum? Can we finish digging the hole in the garden? My metal detector's still beeping and I want to find all the buried treasure, even if it's not pirate."

She kissed his freckled face and his turned up button nose. "Yes, Josh and Poppy will be 'round after lunch to help us to pick all those lovely apples from the tree at the bottom of the orchard. We'll bake a couple of pies, one for Josh's dad and one for us to take back home tonight."

"I want to stay here, Mum. Do we have to go back to the flat tonight? I want to go to school in the village school you showed me. I promise I will be good."

"It's only for another three weeks—just until half term, love. Then we'll come back and live in the cottage until it's sold."

Rebecca smiled down at the person she loved most in the world. For the very first time she felt no coil of guilt, no self-recrimination of her sub-par parenting. The decision she had taken to purchase Rosemary Cottage *had* improved her life and Max's beyond recognition. It had enabled her to meet Josh, which in turn had caused Max to blossom, with the help of Poppy, from the anxious, sleeve-sucking little boy to the bright, confident, animal-loving child he now so clearly was.

And it was not only Max who had flourished. Rebecca could now accept that, with a little help from her friends and *The Little Green Book of Wishes*, she had found the courage to move on, too.

"Do you like Josh, Mum?"

"Yes I do. He's very kind to us." For the first time Rebecca was enjoying the experience of real, unselfish love, but still, she watched Max's reaction to her admission carefully. She was delighted to find intrigue and a soupcon of mischief.

"Do you want to kiss him?"

A FAMILIAR FLIP in her lower abdomen, followed by a tingling sensation rushed through her body as Josh pushed open the picket fence gate. Again, she experienced the melding of passion and comfort from last night.

Carrying a short wooden ladder, greyed with age, over his arm, he and Max marched down the back lawn to the orchard and positioned the ladder onto the gnarled bark of the oldest apple tree. Climbing into its boughs, Josh rained down apples to Max, whose job it was to catch them and pop them into the wicker baskets. Whenever his butterfingers dropped one they both giggled—Max chasing after the apple like a ball boy at Wimbledon.

The warmth of the sun bathed the garden in a golden autumnal glow, casting defused shards of sunlight through the fruit trees. It was one of the most relaxed days Rebecca could remember and she felt a surge of gratitude for Josh. Even if a romantic relationship didn't develop, he had enhanced their lives by his solid, no-hidden-agenda presence.

Max was having the time of his life, too. Fresh air, exercise, and the pursuit of treasure had banished his pale peaky face, in its place was a smiling one sprinkled with freckles. She had no doubts at all about her decision to relocate to Northumberland, her home. But it was time to embark on the long slog back to London.

Josh stuffed the ancient hatchback with their sparse returning belongings, slamming down hard to lock the trunk on the catch on the boot—Rebecca terrified of a repeat performance of the time it flew open on the motorway. She squeezed Max into his booster seat and scooted back up the garden path to check the lock on the heavy oak door.

Josh caught up with her on the doorstep, raising her chin with the tip of his finger to gaze into her emerald eyes. Making sure they were shielded from the road by a rhododendron bush, he kissed her gently.

"The next three weeks will drag without your and Max's company. I will miss you both. Drive carefully and call me when you arrive, no matter what time it is."

"We'll miss you, too, Josh. Thank you for making this such a special weekend and for being so kind to me and Max—for caring about his feelings. He says you're his best Northumberland friend!"

"No higher accolade!" He chuckled.

"Josh, would you be up for attending Deb and Fergus' wedding with me and Max? He's my date of course, but you could tag along." She half joked to ensure he felt no pressure to travel to a marriage of strangers.

"It would be an honour to accompany you both. Thanks, Becky. If I remember correctly, the wedding is being celebrated at the local village hall, isn't it? I'll book into a B&B in the village, if that's okay."

"That'd be great. Well, until the thirty first of October!" And she kissed him on the cheek before jogging happily down the garden path to the car. Rebecca considered performing one of those running skips she'd seen in the movies, where the girl clicks her heels together and joyously fist pumps the air, but she discarded the temptation as she knew she'd probably fall flat on her face.

With Poppy by his side, he raised his arm in a wave from the little wooden gate as she and Max tooted the horn and set off on the first leg of the long journey back to London.

It was this blissful image that remained seared into her mind's eye for the next three weeks.

CHAPTER THIRTY-ONE

THE DAY DAWNED like every other day in Dubai—hot, with the promise of blistering heat to come as the day grew older under the flat blue sky. Cheryl had to admit that after three weeks of the repetitive, uncompromising heat, and despite being an avid sun-worshipper, she found herself scanning the sky for a wisp of cloud, maybe a spell of rain, to escape the monotonous scorch of the sun. Monotony was the word for her life in Dubai.

Bradley's baptism into legal services provision in United Arab Emirates had provided him with a ready-made social life—if one enjoyed socialising with one's colleagues. But Cheryl found that her position as a 'lady of leisure' was not all it was cracked up to be. Filling her endless humdrum days with shopping and spa treatments had initially been immensely enjoyable, but now she craved more than that.

Their sumptuous apartment—leased for them by the law firm—was situated on the thirty-sixth floor of a cutting-edge design, glass monstrosity, but thankfully was air-conditioned to freezing point. Cheryl would never have admitted this to Bradley, who adored the minimalist, sharp lines, and symmetry of the building, but she preferred the black-and-white, mock-Tudor mews they'd shared in London.

All the apartment's furniture, furnishings, and artwork had been provided by the firm's contracted interior-design team, right down to their corporate-blue tea towels and crisp, white bed sheets—three hundred thread count Egyptian cotton. Their attention to intimate details was a little creepy. She'd almost expected to find a selection of fine lingerie in her bedside drawers!

The apartment was immaculate, visited daily by the company's retinue of housemaids who scowled if Cheryl dared to lift a crimson-polished finger, fearing for their continued employment. A chauffeur, Zahid, had been placed at their disposal, available to drive Cheryl where ever the mood took her during the day. But where was that?

She'd shopped 'til she'd dropped', indulging in lightweight linen trousers and sheer, diaphanous summer dresses. Her ebony hair had been coiffed and tousled in one of the many salons. She'd treated herself to a number of spa treatments at several of the luxury hotels' spas, her favourite being Hotel Armani. But, unlike Bradley, she had no work colleagues to team up with and had yet to make any female friends with whom to share her day and her woes.

She found herself mooching around the apartment, avoiding the accusatory stares of the maid—who clearly wanted the place to herself so she could rifle through the wardrobe—waiting for Bradley to return from his day's work. For the last week, the tedious wait had been getting progressively longer, Bradley arriving later and later in an increasingly intoxicated state.

Cheryl now had to admit that she was bored with the sun, bored with the tedium of shopping, and bored with pointless spa treatments. Who would have thought it!

In London, she would by no means have described herself as a culture vulture, but she enjoyed an evening out at a West End show, an occasional visit to the Tate, or the National Portrait Gallery. She adored the escapism of the cinema, too, especially a rom-com with her friends or sister whom she yearned to gossip with and missed tremendously. She'd even admit to having a great time in the corporate box at Chelsea.

But in Dubai? What was there to do here and who did she know to do it with except Bradley, who last night was so incoherent when he arrived back at the apartment, having been drinking since lunchtime—apparently a tradition for a Friday lunch. He'd been unable to escort a dressed-up Cheryl to dinner at the Indian restaurant, Asha, as promised.

They'd argued, culminating in Cheryl launching a crystal vase complete with cream roses—refreshed every day by the maids who had free run of their home—at Bradley, who'd staggered off to the spare room, where he remained, sleeping off the effects of Friday's binge.

It wasn't as if this was anything new. They both over-indulged in London, using Saturday to recover, before resuming their spree on Saturday night. Sundays they passed in a haze of sleep and hangover, recovering their faculties for Monday morning. But in Dubai, Bradley was not including her in his socializing, and she felt not only lonely but also jealous.

Bradley had settled straight away into the ex-pat community and lifestyle. He'd adopted a more relaxed dress code—which she couldn't—accepted the provision of domestic services—which she hated, feeling it invaded her privacy and sense of equality—and as he slaved all day in an air-conditioned office, the oppressive heat didn't seem to bother him, unlike Cheryl who loathed the permanent perspiration and her voluminous hair.

Bradley enjoyed man-bonding and networking accompanied by copious amounts of alcohol, but women held a different place in this society. As he'd returned most evenings intoxicated, they hadn't made love in weeks. In fact, Bradley had shown very little romantic interest in her since they'd arrived.

It was eleven a.m. on a Saturday morning and Cheryl had hoped they could spend some time together, maybe at the tennis club the company had paid their subscription for, along with his colleagues and their wives or partners. It would be an opportunity for Cheryl to make connections and maybe friendships, but Bradley hadn't yet surfaced from their second bedroom.

She stormed into the dim bedroom and shook him awake, noticing his expensive designer suit scrunched on the floor where he'd stepped out of it, and the fact he still wore the pink work shirt from the previous day. This would have been abhorrent to the Bradley in London, who was teased mercilessly for his attention to sartorial detail and meticulous hygiene. An aroma of stale alcohol fumes and vomit pervaded the darkened room.

"Brad, where were you yesterday? What exactly were you drinking? You're disgusting. Will you clean yourself up? I want us to go out. I've been stuck in this clinical box all week. The only company I've had is the maid!"

Groaning, Bradley rolled away from the sharp, piercing light as Cheryl drew back the blinds, revealing vomit stains down the front of his shirt.

"Give it a rest, Cheryl. I don't want to go shopping again and I certainly don't feel like a game of tennis, so don't even suggest going there. I'm spending the day in bed, and then meeting Jacob

[209]

and Marcus at six at the Shark Club. Why don't you go out shopping? Amuse yourself."

Cheryl studied him as though she had never set eyes on him before and was repelled by what she saw. His weekly groomed hair was dishevelled, his eyes bloodshot and grey-rimmed. His five o'clock shadow, usually so attractive, was twenty hours too old, coupled with his crumpled, vomit-splattered shirt. This wasn't the Bradley she knew and loved.

"Are we meeting Marcus and Jacob's wives tonight?"

"No, Cheryl. It's just the lads. We're meeting a couple of potential clients we're hoping are going to put some financial business our way, so no frivolity, I'm afraid. Look, why don't you invite your sister across for a long weekend, just to help you get settled in?"

"Carrie's pregnant, I told you! So she'll loath this heat, too. It's suffocating, and even I can't bear it. And staying in the air-con plays havoc with my skin. I'm so bored here, Bradley, there's nothing to do! I never see you and when I do, you're drunk. It's not fair. This is not what you promised me when I agreed to come here with you."

"Stop whining, Cheryl. This apartment is spectacular. We could never afford anything like this in London. You've got a housemaid, a chauffeur, and money to go shopping for anything you want. Stop being so damn selfish and think about how important it is for me to make a mark here! I've got to be seen around in the right places, get my face known, build up my reputation."

Silent tears drifted down Cheryl's cheeks. She never cried, never had cause to, which stopped Bradley in his self-focused tracks. He pulled her down on the bed and kissed her hard.

"Sorry, Cheryl. I do understand it will take you time to get used to your new life here, but it's a fantastic opportunity. Come on, let's get dressed and I'll escort you out to Adriano's Ristorante, a romantic lunch a deux."

Cheryl would have loved to have told him where he could stick his offer of two hours of his valuable time, but self-interest kicked in as she couldn't stand another day of mooning around the apartment doing nothing. Being alone and the long lonely Saturday night stretched in front of her.

She nodded, slinking away to her bedroom to repair her face and select one of her new flimsy chiffon, ivory tea dresses, decorated with tiny peach rosebuds she'd not had the chance or occasion to wear. Not her usual London attire, but tightly fitted shift dresses and hip-hugging skirts produced an unacceptable level of perspiration, which she loathed.

Zahid drove them to the sumptuous restaurant where they were directed to a pristine, white leather circular booth, their table bedecked with crisp, starched linen and crystal glasses. It was her favourite restaurant, the food was delicious, and she immediately relaxed over her flute of icy vintage rosé champagne, giggling at the anecdotes Bradley was spouting about his new career and work colleagues.

Cheryl hadn't approved of Bradley ordering another bottle of bubbly, hoping to return to their apartment for an afternoon of passionate love-making, her desire for Bradley rekindled, but Bradley had insisted on 'hair of the dog', and reminded her he wasn't driving.

It seemed to do the trick as Bradley morphed into his charismatic, attentive self—stroking her hand, brushing his lips against her earlobe as he whispered slurred words of passion. She felt his desire for her growing, especially as they had not made love for three weeks. As he ran his finger delicately up her inner thigh, her body's response was immediate.

"Not here, Bradley!" She glanced around the packed restaurant. "Come on, let's get back to the apartment." She watched as Bradley knocked back the remainder of their third bottle of champagne. They had paid for it, he'd retorted and struggled up from the table, seizing Cheryl's hand roughly to steady his stance.

As they reached the pristine lobby, Bradley stumbled down the last of the cream-coloured marble steps. He clutched Cheryl to prevent falling, grabbing at the neckline of her flimsy chiffon dress, tearing the delicate material to her waist. As Cheryl had chosen not to wear a bra with the flimsy dress, her pale, pert breasts were immediately exposed to the lobby full of diners waiting for their chauffeurs.

Horrified, Cheryl screamed, shoving Bradley away from her, leaving him sprawling drunkenly on the marble floor, whilst she tried to repair the torn chiffon and resume her dignity, but the front of her dress had torn in tram-lines. Her tears of mortification and Bradley's fumbling at her breasts made matters even more embarrassing for Cheryl and the mesmerised audience, until the maître d' swept over, draping her shoulders with his own jacket as her face burned with humiliation.

Within moments, the police arrived, arrested and handcuffed Bradley, stuffing his disheveled head into the backseat of the patrol car, and drove him straight to Jebel Ali police station and the end of his glittering career.

Zahid arrived to drive Cheryl back to the apartment. She politely asked him to wait whilst she changed into white jeans and an orange t-shirt, stuffed as much as she could into her brand new, matching designer suitcases, and located her passport and credit cards. Zahid sped directly to the airport, Cheryl desperate to escape the month's nightmare she had endured in Dubai.

The knot in her stomach, the lump of rock in her throat, did not unravel or abate until she sank into her allocated seat in Emirates first-class cabin where she spent seven long hours sobbing for her failed relationship. Having terminated the lease on their mews house and resigning from her job at Fortnum and Mason to follow Bradley, she wondered where she went from there.

To her credit, before the Boing 737 had landed at Heathrow, Cheryl's scattered thoughts had turned to Rebecca and Max, and she wasn't beyond realising the similarities of their predicaments at the hands of Bradley Peter Mathews.

BRADLEY SOBERED UP swiftly in the overcrowded cell at Jebel Ali police station as the horror of his situation crashed over him. He'd requested legal representation and his colleague, Marcus, with whom he was due to spend the evening networking, arrived, pristine in his dark business suit, his hangover from the previous evening's exploits untraceable.

"Bradley, you stupid idiot! You know being intoxicated in a public place is a criminal offence in Dubai. There is zero tolerance for drunken behaviour, especially from the ex-pat community. But what were you doing ripping Cheryl's clothes off in the lobby of a restaurant? You caused her to bare her breasts—this is a Muslim country, and you're really in the mire. One of the female diners in the restaurant has made a formal complaint that you have outraged public decency and she was highly offended by witnessing the incident. The best you can hope for is deportation. The worst is a stint in the central prison, which you wouldn't wish on your worst enemy."

Bradley leaned over to his left and vomited into a convenient metal bin. Its polished surface like a mirror, reflecting his handsome face drained of all colour, tinged blue around his jaw. His intelligent, cunning eyes were bloodshot, and a two-day beard was emerging. No sharp, clean edges now—more ruffled tramp.

"I'm not going to any jail, you moron," Bradley spat. "Do your job and get me out of here!"

"I'll do whatever I can for you, Bradley, but you do know that your contract will already have been terminated by the firm. They turn a blind eye to what doesn't go public, but they can never be seen to condone public displays of intoxicated behaviour. I hope you have a Plan B."

"Just get on with getting me out, and ask them to send Cheryl in."

"Cheryl's not here, mate."

"Well, get her on her mobile. Tell her to wait outside with Zahid until you get me out."

Relief flooded Marcus's face as he was handed the opportunity to leave, and he moved toward the door. "It's not what you expected, is it? Not the high-society party capital most people expect. But let me ask you this, did you behave this way in London?"

"Get lost, Marcus."

Bradley spent one month in a prison cell, fearing daily for his life and sexuality, after which he was deported—one of a small but growing band of foreigners who didn't think the rules applied to them.

CHAPTER THIRTY-TWO

HALLOWEEN. A DAY of witches, wizards, and warlocks. Of ghosts, goblins, and ghouls. But not at St Aiden's parish church. A sharp frost had sprinkled the church lawns at dawn with sparkling diamond dew, but the clear blue skies continued to raise the temperature and bathed the pretty village church in warm, late autumn sunshine.

The ladies of the parish had excelled themselves. Lollipop rose bushes in pale ivory—stems tied with cream ribbons—formed a guard of honour along the pathway leading to the heavy, arched church door, which sported a huge wreath of roses and white lilies. Each pew end was adorned with a sprig of holly and gypsophila bound together with ivory bows. The church had achieved the desired 'fairytale' wedding venue.

The congregation chatted noisily, sporadic laughter ringing out as children chased around the pews. Everyone present knew how long Deb and Fergus had waited for this day to arrive and was determined to play their part in making the occasion as momentous and memorable as possible.

The guests were also aware of the bride's disappointment with the kitchen fire at Radley Hall and how the couple's friends had banded together to transform the church hall to as close to Deb's dream wedding as creatively possible. The whole of the previous week had been spent pinning reams and reams of ivory cotton sheeting around the walls, gigantic ivory ribbons and bows dotted the edges, interspersed with flowers from Deb's chosen colour theme of royal purple. The resultant effect was an exact replica of the inside of a luxurious wedding marquee.

Radley Hall had agreed to loan them the octagonal tables and chairs, which they had adorned with starched white linen tablecloths and amazing floral table displays. The Hall had also offered the services of their temporarily redundant chef who had spent a happy three days slaving away in St Aiden's church hall kitchen, whipping up a spectacular wedding feast.

Fergus had whispered to Rebecca during the week that every cloud had a silver lining. He truly believed the church hall was more romantic than the Hall, but most of all, they had saved seven thousand pounds on the reception which meant they could afford the deposit on old Mrs Granville's terraced house on Deb's Mum's street. Although he didn't want to sound unsympathetic, he'd also confided that Mrs Granville would be moving to a local care home after spending one last Christmas in her home.

Rebecca, Josh, and Max parked themselves on the bride's side of the church—left of the aisle near the back—allowing Deb's extended family to take their places at the front. Rebecca gathered and smoothed her peacock-blue silk dress so as not to produce too many creases, pulling the matching short-sleeved jacket closer for warmth. It was warmer outside than in.

[216]

They spotted Nathan holding Millie, who looked so cute in an ivory princess dress, complete with royal purple ribbon sash, her blonde curls tied into a matching purple bow. She was beaming, but nothing could match the pride and joy radiating from Nathan's thin face.

In his best shirt and tie, hair gelled into a quiff at the front, Max looked handsome waiting patiently on the wooden pew, his short legs pointing straight out in front of him. Next to him sat Josh, gorgeous in his charcoal-grey wool suit with royal blue silk lining. Peeping from his cuffs were the rugby ball cufflinks Rebecca had presented him with that morning when she and Max collected him from the B&B, as a small token of thanks for all the hard work he had put in at the cottage's garden. She'd bought a pair for each of his friends, Tom and James, too.

She couldn't prevent herself from flicking glances at him under her eyelashes, his tousled hair shining and his cobalt eyes bright. She felt blessed, perched on the hard bench in this beautiful church, happy in the presence of this gorgeous man and her handsome son. She marvelled at the way her life had changed over the last seven months since meeting the girl of the day, Deborah Marie Bell—soon to be Deborah Marie Horne. Her radiant optimism and enthusiasm, her faith in life, and the power of love and affection had been the driving force behind Rebecca's transformation. She raised her eyes heavenwards and silently thanked the Director of the Fates and Deb from the bottom of her recuperating heart.

She exchanged a smile with Nathan who had also played no small part in her rehabilitation.

Squeezing Josh's hand, she shifted her body closer to him. She didn't forget to thank the wisdom and guidance of the little green book which had taught her to live life as it occured, whatever was thrown at her, and not to straitjacket its experiences into challenges of 'must dos' to be crossed off as quickly as possible in pursuit of the next. Quality of life not quantity was her mantra now.

She and Max had studied the book last night as they snuggled under the duvet. Under the heading of 'Marrying', it had suggested they arrive early, dressed to perfection, and determine to have fun!

She had delivered the completed 'Horne' stained-glass panel to Deb's parents' home the day before and hoped they would love her gift.

An increase in the volume of murmurings bounced from the ancient stone walls. Rebecca swiveled around to gawp at the couple who had just made their grand entrance at the rear of the church.

There was an audible gasp—from Rebecca! The man standing in the stone entrance was an Adonis, exuding charisma from every pore. Olive skinned, immaculately styled, chocolate-brown hair, dark exotic eyes from which he had just removed mirrored designer shades. His slender hips were those of a flamenco dancer, but on this special occasion, they were encased in a beautifully cut, black wool suit, obviously Spanish haute couture, crisp white shirt, and wildly patterned pink and purple silk tie.

After the initial salivation, it was his partner Rebecca couldn't drag her eyes away from.

Lucinda was positively beaming, radiating a warmth Rebecca didn't think she possessed. Her immaculately coiffed bob reflected soft toffee tones, and was slightly longer than she usually wore it. A soft peach, shimmering lip gloss had replaced her normally severe, perfectly applied scarlet lipstick. Rebecca recognised her suit straight away, having drooled over it when she and Deb had been window-shopping at Harrods for wedding ideas to copy.

Lucinda wore an Italian Collezioni, white tweed two piece. The short, pencil-thin skirt skimmed her knee, enhancing her slender tanned legs. The collarless, three-button, open-weave jacket was shot through with a luxurious metallic sparkle thread. But the sparkle of the luscious fabric was nothing compared to the twinkle in its wearer's eyes as she linked arms with her partner.

Rebecca had no difficulty in believing the reason behind the dramatic change in Lucinda's presentation when she resumed her study of the man clutching her hand.

Lucinda spotted them and, continuing with the cornucopia of surprises, made a beeline for the pew behind them, providing Rebecca with the opportunity to clock her shoes—the ivory silk stilettos Deb had salivated over in the bridal boutique. Five-inch heels, peep-toed, ivory satin adorned with minute sparkling crystals.

"May I introduce Raphael? Raph, this is Rebecca and her son, Max," said Lucinda, presenting Max with a dazzling smile. She raised wide questioning eyes to Josh, obviously liking what she saw.

"I'm delighted to meet you, Raphael." Rebecca offered her hand to shake, and was surprised to feel the soft touch of his lips on her hand as he rolled his tongue around her name.

"Enchanted, Rebecca."

Clearing her dry throat, she introduced Josh. The men shook hands and Josh leant forward to kiss Lucinda on her flushed cheeks. Nathan shook hands with Raphael, but shot back to Millie before having to greet Lucinda the same way Josh had, fear lurking behind his eyes.

Rebecca experienced a jolt of suspended reality. This scenario would have been an absurd impossibility two months ago. Thankfully, life does change—occasionally for the worse, but sometimes for the better.

The church organ struck up a crescendo with the first chord of the wedding march. A pale-faced Fergus and his best man, his brother, Alex, stepped forward to await the arrival of his bride.

Rebecca and the congregation spun around in unison to witness Deb float down the narrow aisle, resplendent in her fairy tale wedding dress. The tulle-draped, A-line skirt, scattered with silk petals, so voluminous the sides brushed those lucky guests on the pew ends as she floated toward Fergus. The tight, strapless ivory taffeta bodice, embroidered with delicate sea pearls, suited her figure perfectly. The short train rustled as it swept the stone floor on its journey to the altar where Deb's proud father delivered her hand to her groom.

Deb's ivory veil hung low over her face, but the sheer material couldn't mask her radiant happiness at finally marrying her adored Fergus. She carried single blooms of white lilies, tied with a huge royal purple sash, laid across her arm. Rebecca strained to make out her headpiece, but didn't recognise the Harrods tiara Deb had agonised so long over. The outline of a circlet of flowers poked through her delicate veil and Rebecca hoped to get a better look when Deb drew back the netting.

The couple faced Reverend Briggs, more than ready to make their solemn vows to each other. There wasn't a dry eye when Deb and Fergus read their personally composed poems to each other. Even Josh squeezed Rebecca's hand, offering her his folded cotton handkerchief with Max looking on, his face creased in puzzlement at his mum's tears when he was having such a great time at his first wedding ceremony attendance.

As the new Mr and Mrs Fergus Horne paraded back down the aisle, Rebecca had a chance to catch a glimpse of Deb's crown. Woven bamboo, interspersed with tiny ivory roses and gyp—a perfect replica of the drawing she had made on the firm's expensive cream parchment all those months ago! Its design meant she could wear her flowing pale blonde locks loose in cascading curls, fresh flowers floating around her head like an angel's halo.

Where had she unearthed the precise replica of her dream headpiece, Rebecca marveled. It suited her perfectly. Barefeet would have completed the image, but Rebecca knew she would have never considered this.

And under that spectacular dress were the shoes, those works of art they'd spent an age cooing over. Her most prized possession, she'd admitted in quiet moments, when she had removed them from their box and stroked them.

The congregation filed out of the church, snaking leisurely to the hall next door, most guests agreeing how much more convenient this venue was than the twenty-mile drive which would have been in front of them had Deb and Fergus still been celebrating at Radley Hall.

The happy couple greeted their guests as they entered the transformed church hall, a special word of thanks bestowed on each of them. When Rebecca's turn came, she was grabbed into a tight embrace by Deb, who eyed Josh over her shoulder.

"Gorgeous, Becky. Lucky you!" she whispered in her ear.

Rebecca smiled at her friend's appreciation and good taste, happiness ballooning in her chest. "Congratulations, Deb. You look amazing! All those magazines were well worth their weight in gold. Where did you source that fantastic headpiece? It's the exact replica of your sketch—your perfect design."

"Sam's company, Exquisite Forest, handmade it for me to my detailed spec. She's amazing. And look, I got these earrings from her as a wedding gift." She flicked her immaculately coiffed hair back to reveal hand-crafted, daisy-shaped earrings matching her engagement ring.

[221]

The wedding reception seating plan directed them to a table with Nathan and Millie, Lucinda and Raphael, and Georgina and Jonathan. A few weeks ago, the table plan had presented Deb with an unsolvable conundrum as to where to sit Lucinda and her plus one, but that was no longer an issue. Lucinda was a changed woman and Deb had no qualms seating her with her colleagues from Baringer & Co.

Georgina wore a stunning emerald silk dress with a black, wispy feather fascinator. She looked fabulous, but there was something else playing around her eyes, a sort of smugness. A satisfaction.

Rebecca whispered in her ear as Jonathan pulled out her chair. "Do you have any news you want to spill? You have a glowing expression about you."

Georgina glanced at Jonathan who gave a slight nod, a smile twitching his mouth, a matching smugness in his own grey eyes.

"I'm pregnant!" she whispered.

"Aaah, what fantastic news." She hugged Georgina and kissed Jonathan, realising too late that this overly exuberant greeting was a little bizarre and she had drawn the eagle eye of Lucinda. She flashed an apology at Georgina, about to attempt to cover her tracks.

"It's okay, Becky." She grabbed Jonathan's hand and announced to the table at large, but with her eyes firmly on Lucinda, "Jonathan and I are proud to announce that we are expecting a baby, sometime next May. We're overjoyed!"

"Oh, how wonderful!" Lucinda leapt up and hugged Georgina just as Rebecca had done—Georgina's face a picture over Lucinda's shoulder at the shock of physical contact. "We will discuss your maternity leave package later. I do hope we can accommodate you with part-time hours when you return. Maybe job-share with someone?" Rebecca could have sworn she caught a glint in Lucinda's eye, was she suggesting herself?

Lucinda resumed her seat, Rebecca looking quickly away as she noticed Lucinda smooth her palm up and down Raphael's stretched thigh under the table. He favoured her with a luscious smile as Rebecca witnessed first-hand the chemistry between them.

The wedding feast was superb, Radley Hall's loaned chef excelling himself. The chef had pulled out all the stops for the wedding meal. He'd explained to anyone who complimented his expertise that he'd been bored witless without the use of his beloved kitchen at the Hall and spent the time experimenting with new recipes and flavours.

The company was relaxed and friendly, the conversation fascinating as Lucinda and Raphael chatted about her sister's recent wedding, the unusual customs of a Spanish wedding compared to an English one, and Lucinda's idyllic week spent on Raphael's yacht moored in the marina at Palma, to which they intended to return immediately after the wedding on his chartered helicopter. It was as though they had stepped from the pages of a glossy magazine, a lifestyle inaccessible even to a partner in a top law firm. Lucky Lucinda!

Max, Millie, and the many other children invited to the wedding were entertained by a magician and puppeteer. Spurts of laughter and shrieking erupted from time to time from the blue and pink spotted rug he had set out on which they sat cross-legged like obedient puppies.

After the speeches, the tables were cleared away into waiting vans to be returned to Radley Hall, and the hall was prepared for the onslaught of the live indie band made up of Fergus's old school friends.

[223]

For such a tall, broad guy, Josh was a surprisingly nimble dancer. Rebecca laughed and giggled her way through the rest of the evening at the ridiculous moves he and Max performed, each trying to outdo the other in the choreography stakes. She loved seeing them have such fun together, but she did frequently have to drag her eyes away from the snaking hips of Raphael, his dance moves scoring a perfect ten. Wow!

At nine p.m. on the dot, the party paused as the guests gathered at the church's kissing gate to send an ecstatic couple off on their honeymoon to Paris, staying in five-star luxury with Fergus promising a celebratory dinner and champagne at the restaurant at the top of the Eiffel Tower. Deb had melted into floods of tears when he disclosed their hotel destination, having dreamed of vacationing at the French sister hotel in London for years.

Max and Millie gleefully launched handfuls of rice like pellets, not just at the bride and groom but the whole gathering, and then chased each other giggling around the churchyard. Rebecca turned to Josh to comment on the fantastic evening, but found him studying her with an intensity that took her breath away.

Checking to make sure Max was out of sight, he lowered his head and kissed her gently on her moist lips. "Rebecca Mathews, you are gorgeous."

She saw Georgina watching them, flashing her a 'well done' smile. She moved away from Josh to wave a final farewell to Deb as a sprig of flowers sailed through the air toward her. She reached up to catch it.

Josh bent down and swept her into his strong arms, swinging her around and around, laughing as a small voice shouted, "My turn, my turn, my turn, swing me, too, Josh!" He deposited Rebecca onto her unsteady feet and grabbed Max's little pudgy hands in his own strong ones, swinging him in a wide circle as Max squealed, "Yes, yes, yes."

CHAPTER THIRTY-THREE

BRADLEY PUNCHED IN Rebecca's number, clutched the phone tightly while scratching his unshaven chin and running his trembling fingers through his too-long hair.

He no longer had the money for a regular haircut. In fact, since his release from the living hell of the Dubai jail and his subsequent inevitable dismissal from his employment, he had no income at all. Now that he had a criminal record and his reputation and integrity were in shreds, he knew that no law firm would touch him. Was this how Rebecca had felt when she had been suspended from practice?

An unexpected coil of sympathy and shame snaked around Bradley's chest, but he nudged it away.

Cheryl had refused to see him and the lease on their mews home had been terminated. As he had nowhere else to live, he'd been forced into the humiliating position of confessing his shame to his horrified parents and begging his mother to allow him to return to his childhood bedroom.

His father had refused, mortified that his son should have sunk to such depths. No one in the family had ever had any contact with law enforcement, not even a parking violation, Gordon Matthews had repeatedly reminded Bradley.

His mother had relented, as he knew she would, but it was painful to see her disappointment and his father's disgust written clearly across their faces whenever their paths crossed. He had to get away from their silent reprimands and Rebecca would be that ticket.

"Hello?"

"Hi, Rebecca, it's me." Bradley's smooth tones resonated through the telephone line.

"What do you want, Bradley?" She sighed.

"What sort of greeting is that, Becky?"

"Becky? You've never called me that."

"I'm just calling to let you know I'm in Newcastle. I have some free time to meet up with you. To talk about our future."

"Our future? What's going on, Bradley? And why are you in the area? I thought you were busy living the high life with Cheryl in Dubai?"

"Well that didn't exactly work out as I'd hoped. If you want to hear me say it, I admit I got caught up in the whole 'networking until you drop' scene out there. I was the new guy. I needed to make my mark. Overindulged, I suppose. So I'm back in the UK. Cheryl and I are no longer an item so I thought I'd come up to the cottage for a few days. We can talk. I can even take Max off your hands for a few hours." Bradley was shocked to hear the tremble in his voice as an unidentifiable burst of emotion sprang to his throat when he mentioned his son.

[227]

"Take Max off my hands? Max is not and never has been a burden to be relieved, Bradley!"

"Is everything okay, Becky?" A man's concerned voice came over the phone.

"Who's that?" Bradley snapped.

"It's none of your business, Bradley. And no, you cannot come across to my cottage. You gave up your chance to *talk* about our future a long time ago. I'm happy to report that I have moved on and I recommend you do the same."

"But Max is my son..." Bradley began, horrified to hear a whine of desperation in his voice.

"You have never been a father to Max, Bradley. Should Max ask to see you then I will contact you via your parents, but I wouldn't hold your breath. Your neglect of your responsibilities as a parent has repercussions. Max rarely asks about you. Your behaviour toward him has ensured that you are a stranger to him. Now, unless you have anything else to say—"

Bradley sank into the hideous chintzy sofa his mother had owned since he was a young boy. A tear trickled down his cheek as, for the first time in years, he realised he had run out of options.

WRAPPED IN THICK, hand-knitted sweaters, Josh and Rebecca hugged steaming mugs of hot chocolate and relaxed on the greying wooden patio. The outdoor heater blazed as they surveyed the now-barren back garden of Rosemary Cottage. Rebecca's love for the cottage grew as the house travelled through the changing seasons, each revealing different special surprises.

It was only a week until Christmas and Max was hyper. It was his first Christmas in a house with a real chimney for Santa to descend with his bountiful sack.

He'd settled well into the local village school and made a firm friend and partner in crime, Ollie, who had already visited the cottage for tea and a personal guided tour of the treasure trove at the bottom of the orchard. Max had declared that whilst he loved the teachers and Ollie, the best bit of his new school life was seeing his mum waiting for him at the school gate as he shot out from classes not a minute past three fifteen.

One weekend, Josh had patched up the roof for the winter months with the help of his friend Tom, whose fiancée, Hilary, had proved to be a welcome guest for dinner that night. She was a nurse at the Royal Victoria Infirmary in Newcastle and regaled them with some hysterical anecdotes. They'd enjoyed an evening of free-flowing wine and good company huddled around the warmth of the Aga at the pine kitchen table—mismatched chairs, plates, and glasses adding to the relaxed ambience.

Rebecca prayed the roof would hold out until the cottage sold, which it showed no sign of doing to date. Although dreading that day, its sale would provide her with a clean slate financially.

Deb and Fergus had just left, having spent the weekend at Rosemary Cottage and declaring it to be idyllic. Fergus and Josh had taken Max up to the farm, allowing Deb and Rebecca girl time to catch up on all the gossip.

"Georgina was gob-smacked when Lucinda called her into the hallowed corner office to discuss her maternity leave with her. She almost pled with her to consider returning to the firm three days a week," Deb had told Rebecca. "But the shock was that she offered Georgina a partnership on a job-share basis with herself, as she intended to spend extended weekends in Palma with Raphael!" Deb smirked.

Lucinda had expressed her sadness at the loss of Rebecca, whom she admitted to engaging in April because she'd respected her as a talented advocate and had enjoyed locking horns with her during previous dealings when Rebecca worked at Harvey & Co. She desperately needed to retain Georgina's talents at Baringer. Rebecca's heart softened further for the re-born Lucinda.

"And you'll never guess what else she admitted to Georgina. Lucinda had overheard one of our many conversations extolling the virtues of your *Little Green Book of Wishes*. Like any astute lawyer of her calibre would, she had indulged in a copy to see what all the hilarity was about. Do you know what I think, Becky? Maybe Lucinda just wanted to be part of our happy coterie, but her position as partner prevented it." Deb's heart was large enough to overlook her boss's many unreasonable traits.

"What do you want to bet that she devoured its gems of wisdom and resolved to try out some of its suggestions at her sister's wedding? The little green book delivered Raphael." Deb dissolved into fits of giggles.

Rebecca snuggled closer to Josh, sipping her hot chocolate and smiled at the memory. Deb had been thrilled when Rebecca showed her how her newly formed interior designing business was thriving. She'd converted the barns at High Matfen Farm, each one showcasing diverse designs and Rebecca had been amazed that the traditional design—with modern gas-powered sky blue Aga, farmhouse-style kitchen, stenciling dotted around the bathroom— had sold first and not the contemporary, muted beige and cream leather of the more modern design. She eagerly anticipated her creative juices being let loose on Josh's four new properties, due to be completed early in the New Year.

She'd also fulfilled her silent promise to George by spending one afternoon a week reading daily newspapers and cherished books to the residents at St Oswald's Lodge, and assisting those who needed a little support in managing a cup of tea or homemade scone.

A terracotta urn, filled with myriad fragrant herbs from Rosemary Cottage's garden, had been donated to the Lodge in George's memory and Rebecca enjoyed sharing the different aromas with the residents whilst they took a constitutional around the garden.

"I was waiting until I got you alone to make this announcement," ventured Josh, sipping his hot chocolate. "We can tell Max in the morning, but I knew he would have been so excited he'd never have gone to sleep."

Rebecca's stomach gave a twist and she held her breath.

"That muddy disc of metal we unearthed in September. As you know Tom showed it to his colleague at the university. This morning, Professor Hicks called to confirm that it *is* a coin from the Roman era when this area around Hadrian's Wall was occupied. Most bronze coins are not very valuable, as quite a few have been found. Apparently you can pick some of them up on an auction site for five pounds, would you believe."

He paused, grasped Rebecca's cold fingers, drawing her closer into his arms. "But your coin—remember how its face depicted the bearded Emperor Hadrian on horseback addressing his troops, clear as the day it was struck? Well, Professor Hicks reckons its value could be upwards of forty thousand pounds! He was as excited as I've ever heard a fifty-year-old historian. He has asked for your permission to e-mail photographs of the coin to his friend at the British Museum, as they recently had a similar coin on public display, and then he will be able to give a more precise valuation." He watched her face as realisation dawned.

"If we decide to sell the coin, is the money ours? Do we own this coin?"

"Yes, you found it, well, Max did, on your land. As it's bronze and not gold or silver and as you only found one, then I'm sure the find doesn't fall under the Treasure Trove rule. But Prof Hicks will check the legal situation out with his pal at the British Museum as some finds have to be referred to the Coroner," Josh explained.

"If you sold the coin, Becky, it would mean you could stay in Rosemary Cottage. I know how much the place means to you. You could pay back all the money to the bank and your dad's care fees, even apply to be restored to the Solicitors Roll, if that's what you want," he said earnestly.

She was silent for a few moments, drinking in his eager, happy face. "I love you, Joshua Andrew Charlton."

"I love you, too, Rebecca Jane Mathews, but I'm thinking I could love Rebecca Jane Charlton even more!"

She fell into his strong, welcoming arms.

As they kissed in the moonlight, neither of them paused to notice *The Little Green Book of Wishes* perched on the kitchen window ledge, discarded. Its work here was done!

ABOUT THE AUTHOR

Lindsey Paley is a Yorkshire girl who now lives in North East England with her husband and young son. When not writing in her peppermint and cream summerhouse (shed), she can be found either up to her elbows in flour baking cakes and biscuits or practicing her swing on the golf course.

The Wish List Addiction is Lindsey's third novel.

If you were inspired by Rebecca's lists, Lindsey would love to hear what's on your 'Wish List' or 'Bucket List'. Please contact her on her Author Facebook page https://www.facebook.com/lindseypaleybooks.

Thank you for your Prism Book Group purchase! Visit our website to enjoy free reads, great deals, and entertaining, wholesome fiction!

Made in the USA
Charleston, SC
03 December 2014